Pleasing
Mr. Sutton

West Coast, Book 5

Jasmine Haynes

Redwood
Valley
Publishing

He has only one rule. She will do everything he says exactly when he tells her to do it.

Chairman of the board Rance Sutton is looking for a new playmate, an untried submissive he can train to do things his wicked way.

Miss Dawson, the chairman's personal secretary, wants to get a lot more personal. What better way than becoming his new submissive? After all, she already does everything his way. So really, what's a little naughty discipline if the payoff is Mr. Sutton in her bed? And that's something she's dreamed about for the entire five years she's worked for him.

The problem? This will be no love affair. He will be her dom. And she will be his submissive. Miss Dawson's desires aren't part of the bargain; everything will be about pleasing Mr. Sutton...

Author Note: This book contains explicit sexual material including multiple partners.

Join Jennifer and Jasmine's newsletter for free books and notice of new releases, plus exclusive content and contests: http://bit.ly/SkullyNews

ACKNOWLEDGMENTS

Thanks to my special network of friends who support me, brainstorm with me, and encourage me: Bella Andre, Shelley Bates, Jenny Andersen, Jackie Yau, Ellen Higuchi, Kathy Coatney, Pamela Fryer, Rosemary Gunn, and Laurel Jacobson. Thanks to Clio and Cody Alston for all their input and help. A special thanks to Rae for such great covers! And of course, as always, I appreciate everything my husband does to help make my writing career flourish and my life easier.

CHAPTER ONE

"Miss Dawson, your number one task this week is to find a new submissive for me."

"Excuse me?" Monica Dawson stared at her boss, Rance Sutton, businessman, entrepreneur, investor, and board member for several multinational conglomerates, both large and small scale. She held the position of personal secretary to him. But he'd never gotten *this* personal.

"I assume there are websites where you can post my requirements," he suggested.

His body toned from daily workouts, Mr. Sutton was an extremely attractive man. Monica was tall in her ubiquitous high heels, but he topped her by at least two inches. At forty-nine, he looked a good five years younger, his short hair a dark shade of blond that masked any gray except for a few strands at his temple. Even those you could only make out if you got close enough. Which she sometimes did when she came around the desk to lay out a contract for him or point to a pertinent item in a document. She liked being near him.

To this request, though, she had no idea what to say. "Uh, yes, well…" Sure there was online dating, but a site for connecting submissives with doms?

The office suite was housed in a high-rise building. Mr. Sutton's domain was decorated like an English country gentleman's study, the huge masculine desk, thick Persian rugs, dark wood paneling, bookcases packed with leather bindings, a marble fireplace surrounded by a comfortable sofa and wing chairs. The modern exception was the large flat-panel TV over the fireplace mantel, which Mr. Sutton kept tuned to a financial channel. The midmorning sun poured through the floor-to-ceiling windows overlooking skyscrapers and San Francisco Bay. Despite the energy-efficient windows provided by West Coast Manufacturing, where Mr. Sutton sat as chairman of the board, Monica felt her skin heating. She often felt warmer in his presence, but this was different, a mixture of embarrassment, disbelief, and irritation.

Standing on the opposite side of his big leather-topped desk, he executed a nonchalant wave of his hand. "Do a search, Miss Dawson. I have no doubt that with your skills you'll find the right candidate. Here are my prerequisites." He flipped around a paper that had been lying on the desk. "I'm looking for a woman who is intrigued by the lifestyle but hasn't yet dabbled. I find the idea of breaking in a newbie exciting." He dropped his voice, not a whisper, but something that sent a zing along her nerve endings. "I want to teach her to live and breathe for what I can give her."

Monica's heart rate rose, her skin flushed, and it was suddenly hard to catch her breath. Maybe it was the intensity in his gaze, the timbre of his voice, or the words themselves.

She'd been his secretary for five years. Day in and day out, she'd lived and breathed her job, and he paid her handsomely. But she wanted things from him beyond money. Things she'd fantasized about.

Except that she was his employee. He had women, several. They were arm candy. And sometimes a bit more, though there were never any serious girlfriends with staying power. Monica was used to buying trinkets for those lady friends. She'd even gone to an exclusive store near Union

Square that catered to his sexual tastes and purchased various toys. Sex toys. She was used to that, too. She was, after all, his *personal* secretary and Mr. Sutton took that literally. But this was beyond belief.

So she wanted to be very clear about this task. "So you want me to post an online personal ad for a submissive. And then what? Do you want me to vet the candidates?"

Mr. Sutton laughed. "Just weed out the ones who don't meet my criteria." He tapped the single sheet of paper in front of him, then pushed it closer. "It's all very clear."

She picked up the document gingerly, as if it might sting her like a nettle. There were no height or weight measurements, merely that the woman be meticulous about her appearance and make the most of her assets, whatever those may be. The age range was between thirty-five and sixty. At thirty-eight, Monica was at least in his lower range.

She glanced up. "Sixty?"

Mr. Sutton smiled. "A mature woman has fewer inhibitions and limitations."

"But don't women lose interest in sex after they reach menopause?"

He laughed, shaking his head. Mr. Sutton often laughed, with fine lines at his eyes that made him even more appealing. "You are so young, my dear." There was only the slightest hint of condescension in his tone. "It all depends on the woman. Many experience heightened desire. It just needs to be cultivated."

Her skin twitched at the idea of Mr. Sutton *cultivating*.

He fluttered his hand at her. "Read on."

No prior bondage or discipline experience, but a healthy desire to explore all the possibilities including spanking, restraint, blindfold, and various other forms of BDSM. Be willing to accept punishment. No fears or limits.

Well, the last certainly eliminated her. "That's all?"

"Is there anything you think should be added?"

There were a lot of things she'd like to add, but she took a deep breath and said, "Do you want me to put anything about you in the ad?" If the potential candidates knew he was a multimillionaire, they would flock to him in droves. There'd be so much weeding to do, they'd have to hire another assistant to handle her other duties.

"Just say a middle-aged dom looking to train a newbie."

"Middle-aged?" She said that aloud, with more than a hint of incredulity. There was nothing middle-aged about Mr. Sutton. He was in his prime.

"I make no bones about my age, Miss Dawson. A woman who's interested in delving into the daunting world of BDSM will want a man with experience."

She *almost* groaned aloud, and the irritation was no longer a mere flash. She was downright seething with it.

How dare he ask her to find another woman for him? Didn't he know *anything*? Was he so blind? Or had his head been buried in the sand? Didn't he see *her* standing right in front of him?

Or did he simply find her unattractive?

She clutched his list to her chest. "I'll start the search immediately, Mr. Sutton."

"Thank you, Miss Dawson."

She turned so fast on her heel that she came close to stumbling. And she did *not* stumble on her heels. Ever.

She'd always dreamed about him. His sexual kicks intrigued her. The more explicit the purchase he had her make, the more tantalizing her fantasies grew. And the more tempting Mr. Sutton became. She loved her job, enjoyed working for him. There was travel and interesting people. Though he treated her with the utmost professionalism, he was also quite open with her about his predilections. She'd researched him before applying, and she'd known the job was a perfect match. She liked to think he could no longer manage without her.

Monica already lived and breathed Mr. Sutton. She wanted him for herself, and she'd be damned if she'd let some other woman be the newbie he broke in.

Rance Sutton watched Miss Dawson stride the length of the Persian carpet. With her back to him as she left, he allowed himself a delightful perusal of her gently swaying hips.

Miss Dawson had an exceptional rear view.

The high-waisted, pencil-slim skirt hugged her curves, and one more button than strictly professional had slipped the moorings of her white blouse, revealing a hint of creamy cleavage. The high heels set off her long legs to perfection, and the tendrils of blond hair that had slipped loose from the knot at her nape teased his senses.

Unfortunately, she was off limits. She was too good at her job to muddy the waters with sexual gratification. He could find that anywhere, but an exceptional personal secretary was priceless.

She closed the door quietly. Too quietly? Perhaps. He'd informed her right from the beginning that she would be required to perform some tasks that would be of a personal nature. She'd never balked. She hadn't exactly balked now, but he'd detected a certain edge. He wasn't asking her to *procure* for him, but simply to list an ad. And cull the responses. He'd subjected her to worse.

He simple didn't have the time—or patience—for the task.

Quite frankly, he was bored with the state of his sex life. The women in his sphere were either high society and high maintenance, or jaded submissives. He needed fresh meat, so to speak. A woman to train in his ways. The thought got his blood pumping almost as much as the sight of Miss Dawson's retreating ass did. He needed something new, something exciting.

Miss Dawson would find the perfect fit. She always did.

"I don't know how you can put up working for a man who would ask you to upload a sex ad for him. It's totally demeaning." Sean propped his feet on the coffee table in the flat they shared. The place had pure San Francisco character, crown moldings, wood floors, a bay window.

"It's no different from having me buy an O-ring gag." Monica hadn't found that demeaning, although she was probably the only woman on the face of the planet who wouldn't. She'd had to look up the device on the Internet to figure out how it was used. In fact, she'd read quite a bit about bondage and submission on the web. The research had given her the oddest thrill. She'd imagined herself on her knees, at Mr. Sutton's mercy, her hands tied behind her back, her mouth gagged with a ring through which he fed her every inch of his massive...

She was getting wet. Just like she'd been the day she'd bought the O-ring gag. And today, despite her irritation, when Mr. Sutton explained what he wanted.

"You *are* a submissive." Disgust edged Sean's tone.

Sean Kennedy had been her best friend since high school, which was why they could say just about anything to each other. And why she'd revealed everything about Mr. Sutton right from that first job interview five years ago. They didn't have the same taste in men. Sean preferred preppy, white-collar types their own age whereas she liked authoritative, older executives. Like Mr. Sutton. Sean wasn't currently in a relationship, but he'd found someone at work who'd piqued his interest. Unfortunately, the guy was still in the closet. With his thick, curly black hair, green eyes, long lashes, and wicked grin, Sean was exceptionally good-looking. He was average height—Monica was actually taller in her heels—but that was the only thing average about Sean. Woe-is-me to many a girl when she learned he was gay.

"Sweetie, don't you get that having you buy sex toys is crossing the line?"

She made a face. "It makes you hot, too. That's why you

always want to know what new toy he's had me purchase."
Seated on the opposite end of the flower-print sofa, Monica
had stripped out of her work attire in favor of shorts and a
tank top in deference to the August heat. After a couple of
days of this hot weather, the fog would roll in off the bay to
cool things down.

Sean shot her a wicked grin. "Just because that dirty
device made us *both* hot doesn't mean Sutton is good for
you. What the hell do you want from the man anyway?"

She couldn't say *love*. She had strong feelings for Mr.
Sutton, but she couldn't define them. Maybe she just wanted
the whole Cinderella thing, where she was suddenly
transformed in the handsome prince's eyes, and he swept
her off her feet. She wanted to play out a fantasy, more than
one fantasy. Secretly she wanted to cede all control, for a
period of time, to a man as powerful and authoritative as
Mr. Sutton. Just to see what it felt like.

Of course she wasn't going to say all that to Sean. There
was revealing everything, and then there was baring her soul.
"I want to experience sexy new things I've never tried. And
you know I've always found him appealing."

"Right," Sean said drily. "Which is why you researched
him before the interview."

"I researched him to make sure I'd like working for
him." And because she'd seen him in the society pages and
found him highly attractive.

Sean took a long pull on his beer. "Sweetie, I'm only
saying this because I love you and I don't want to see you
get hurt. But you know he'll use you up and spit you out."

"It's not like I'm going to fall in love with him." She
made the denial to throw Sean off the scent of her emotions.
"I just want a taste." Of him. Of the devilish things he did
to his women. She wanted to see what it was like to let Mr.
Sutton take over.

Sean gave her a look. "You're too good for him. He's a
two-time loser at marriage."

"That wasn't his fault. Both his wives cheated on him."

Sean pressed his lips together and dipped his head to look at her through lashes so lush any girl would be jealous. "And don't you think there's a reason why?"

She couldn't imagine why any woman in her right mind would cheat on Mr. Sutton. "So you're going to blame the victim."

"I'm just saying there's two sides to every story." He cocked his head. "And please, no self-respecting boss asks his employee to buy his gifts for him. That went out in the eighties."

"He's never asked me to buy gifts for his mother or his sister." He was very respectful of his family. "What I buy for him aren't *gifts*." Though she didn't exactly know what to call the toys she purchased.

"It's sexual harassment."

Except that Mr. Sutton never did anything untoward, not when he told her what to buy nor when she returned to hand him the purchase. He didn't explain its purpose or make a reference to wanting to try it on her, and he never mentioned the lady's name to whom he planned to give it. It was almost as if he'd sent her out to buy a box of chocolates.

The truth was she sometimes wanted more of a reaction from Mr. Sutton. She wanted him to ask if she'd ever used a dildo or sex beads or a flogger. Or the gag. Something, *anything*, to acknowledge that he saw her as more than his secretary.

"I don't agree with that assessment," she said stubbornly.

"He's autocratic and dictatorial. A throwback."

Monica couldn't disagree, but those weren't necessarily bad things.

"Misogynistic."

"He's not. He reveres women."

"Right. That why he uses handcuffs, blindfolds, gags, and floggers on them."

"I never should have told you about the stuff he's asked

me to buy. I should have known you'd throw it back in my face."

Sean was on a roll. "He doesn't *pay* you enough to do all that."

"He pays me very well," she protested.

"And that's why you have to share a flat with me. You're paid so well, and you *voluntarily* have a roommate."

"I'll have you know I love my roommate. And I love living in San Francisco as much as you do." She didn't own a car. There was always Bart or Muni or a cable car to go anywhere she wanted. Something was always happening in the city. She loved people-watching. She loved the noise and the bustle, the nightlife, the constant activity. "I can't imagine living in the East Bay or on the Peninsula." Though Sean worked down on the Peninsula, he wouldn't dream of living there either. But neither of them could afford to live in the city alone unless they shared, especially not in their gorgeous walk-up with its two master suites. That was worth any price, even if the rooms weren't terribly large. "You're just arguing for the sake of arguing."

Sean smiled slightly. "I might be exaggerating, but there's a core of truth." He reached out to wiggle her big toe. "Your taste in men is terrible, and I don't want to see my best friend get hurt. Haven't I always looked out for you?"

"Like a big brother." He loved her, and no man was good enough for her. Which he was always quick to point out when she began dating a new guy. "You know me too well."

"That's why I'm not wrong about this."

She gave him a steady gaze. "But that would be assuming I wanted a relationship. And all I really want is sexual adventure."

"Why don't I believe you?"

Monica tried not to squirm. "I have no idea why. I've thought about this for a long time, and now is my opportunity."

"What if he turns you down?"

She shrugged despite the flutter in her belly. "Then he turns me down and I'm still just his secretary."

"And what if he accepts? What are you going to do when it's over? Because I guarantee you won't have a job anymore."

She took a deep breath before answering. "I'll find another one. But I'd rather take the risk than never know what it's like." She wanted to know, *had* to know. Mr. Sutton and all his wicked ways were worth risking her job.

So tomorrow, she would answer his ad for a new submissive.

CHAPTER TWO

"I have the perfect candidate for the new position."
Monica placed the resume on his big desk and slid it across
to him. She'd given herself an hour to prepare before
presenting it. That hour had also given Mr. Sutton a chance
to enjoy his first cup of coffee, a special blend she brewed
him. He'd be mellower now.

"That was fast work." He remained seated while she
stood before him. It seemed submissive, like the teenage girl
who's forced to stand before the headmaster.

"The choice ended up being quite easy." She laced her
fingers behind her back. Again there was a submissive feel
to the gesture. She'd dressed for him. Her blouse was teal,
sheer with a lacy camisole beneath, which she'd paired with
a cream skirt that hugged her behind, but dropped tastefully
to below the knees. She felt sexy but tailored, classy but
inviting.

"Commendable work," he said, picking up the resume.

Her tension began to rise as he read. She'd addressed
every bullet point on his list. She was intrigued by the
lifestyle, she'd never dabbled, she wanted him to teach her,

she was willing to accept pain to receive pleasure, she needed his punishment, and so on. His eyes flicked back and forth across the page, but not another muscle twitched. Until finally he laid the single sheet of paper back on the expensively tooled leather top of his desk.

"You already have a job, Miss Dawson."

She willed her cheeks not to flame. "Yes. But as I assume this new *position*"—she flexed the word, adding a sexual spin—"will be extracurricular, I believe I can carry out both functions to your complete satisfaction."

He watched her unblinkingly, and the temperature in the office began to rise. A flush started inside, rushing out to her skin. He had to notice the scarlet blaze.

"I have no doubt about your abilities, but it's never good to mix business and pleasure. We have a professional relationship. Making you my submissive would violate that."

A kernel of ice expanded in her chest. He was turning her down.

"This is not the kind of thing you can turn on and off, Miss Dawson. I think it's best—"

She couldn't let him reject her. "A lot of people might consider that asking me to buy sex toys for you is violating our business relationship."

"You are my *personal* secretary. I never asked you to demonstrate the devices for me."

"In a corporate environment, the CEO doesn't ask his secretary to search for submissive playmates." She'd been about to cite Holt Montgomery, CEO of West Coast Manufacturing, as an example, but he was marrying his secretary next month, so that comparison might fall short.

"I mentioned when I hired you that some of the tasks I gave you would be of a more personal nature." His face was implacable. Unreadable. Mr. Sutton could be a hard man when he chose. Last night's bravado was starting to fade.

But if she backed down now, there would never be another chance. Just the fact that she'd asked had changed their working relationship. How would she get over the embarrassment, let alone the rejection? She'd made the choice, now she had to convince him.

"There are advantages you might not have thought of," she told him. "Except when you have meetings or when we're traveling"—she accompanied him and took care of the details—"we're alone in this suite all day." She flourished a hand to encompass his office, her smaller accommodations outside, and the conference room. "You must have thought about having a submissive you can command during the day." She lowered her voice. "Make her do anything. Right here." She lovingly stroked the desk's leather top. "Or over there." She pointed to the sofa.

She imagined herself splayed out on that genteel couch. Or facedown on his desk while he did all those mysterious dominant things to her. "Anything," she said softly. "Anywhere."

His nostrils flared slightly, the first indication of an emotion. "Miss Dawson."

She wouldn't let him stop her. "Every time you send me out to buy one of those *devices*"—she drew out the word for effect—"I'm dying to know exactly what you do with them." She moistened her lips. "How it would feel."

He swallowed, his Adam's apple gliding slowly along his throat. "Miss Dawson." It was all he seemed capable of saying.

How far could she go? She'd waited a long time for this opportunity. She'd go to great lengths to make it happen.

So she told him the truth, in a soft sexual purr meant for the bedroom. "And every time it makes me wet."

❧

Holy hell. She'd made him as hard as the steel holding up the Golden Gate.

He wanted her now. Instantly. Bent over his desk. His hand on her ass, turning her flesh pink with a well-deserved spanking. Just before he drove deep inside her.

Rance Sutton allowed himself a deep breath. He remained seated behind his desk, disguising the power her words had over him. He had too much restraint to act on his base instincts in the moment. Instead, he found the control to conduct a cost-benefit analysis.

If he made her his submissive and it didn't work out, he'd lose the best secretary he'd ever had. He had no illusions that she would stay on once the sexual nature of their relationship ended. It would be too awkward for her. And women tended to get emotional. No, she'd leave him. After five years of perfect order in his life, he'd have to train a new secretary. It was much easier to break in a submissive. It was a ridiculous idea. Potentially life-altering. Was making Miss Dawson his submissive worth everything he could lose? The answer took only a heartbeat.

Hell, yes.

Her blouse was see-through to the lacy garment beneath, making a man ache for more. Not that *he* ached, he had too much control for that. On the face of it, her skirt was circumspect, below the knee, but it molded to her hips, cupped her ass, and begged to be lifted for a good spanking. He imagined the heat of her flesh against his palm.

Most fucking definitely yes, she was worth it.

He stood abruptly, buttoned his suit jacket as if he were a TV lawyer preparing to give his opening statement, and marched around the desk. He liked that she was tall. He enjoyed her endless legs.

And now she would become his.

As he towered over her, the morning sun backlighting her so that she appeared to be nothing more than a silhouette, he said, "A trial run. You have two seconds to agree. Or retreat to your desk."

The bright light behind her obscured the workings of her face. He counted three seconds before she spoke. "I agree."

The words went through him like an electric charge. "Stand over there, face me."

He pointed three feet behind her, halfway between the

back of the sofa and the windows. When she was in position, he circled her. Scented her. Sweet. Aroused. Oh yes, she was wet.

He stopped, moved back to the windows. Now he was the silhouette, her face plainly in view. She was a good-looking woman with symmetrical features, not gorgeous, but extremely appealing to him. Her breasts were large, her hips shapely, curvy in all the right places. She wasn't skin and bones, and he was a man who liked his meat.

"I have only one rule," he told her.

Her hazel eyes, the usually ordinary color now dusted with gold, widened.

"You will do anything I tell you to do precisely when I tell you to do it."

She swallowed, inhaled, exhaled, plumping her magnificent breasts with each breath.

"Nod once."

She nodded. Her earrings bounced, a ray of sun turning the abalone shell iridescent.

She'd opened his eyes. He saw a woman. He drew in her musk. He smelled her sex. There was no going back. She wanted to learn. And he was so going to enjoy teaching her.

"Your training begins now. Lock the door."

She tipped her head a scant fraction of a centimeter and her lips curved infinitesimally. "I already locked it."

Naughty girl. She needed to be taught who had the upper hand.

"Take off your clothes."

⊚

Monica froze. She hadn't been sure what to expect, but immediate nakedness wasn't the first thing that came to mind. She would be utterly exposed.

"Was there something unclear about my instruction?" His voice was soft yet unyielding.

"But we're in front of the windows," she whispered. As

15

if he hadn't specifically positioned her within view of the skyscrapers opposite. "Someone might see." Although the reflection on the outside would probably render them invisible.

"Our new relationship requires that you will be naked in front of an audience when I chose for you to be. So you'd better get used to it now."

Monica did not let her teeth chatter. She would not show her nerves physically. She knew doms took their submissives to clubs. In the heat of the night, the thought had made her wet.

"Miss Dawson," he said in that soft voice. "Whether you are seen or not isn't important. What's important is that you obey. That is the first thing you must learn." He dropped his voice to a deadly note. "Whatever I say whenever I say it."

She'd asked for this. And she'd have it. She'd have *him*. Monica unbuttoned her blouse and let it slide off her arms.

By the time she'd pulled the hem of her camisole from her skirt, her nipples were hard. And Mr. Sutton's normally light blue eyes appeared as dark as velvety midnight.

"You naughty girl, Miss Dawson. You're not wearing a bra."

She'd given him her resume, so why not be honest about the rest? "I wanted to entice you."

"You most certainly did."

Did that mean he knew she'd wanted to entice him? Or that he'd actually been enticed?

He waggled a finger. "More."

She tried stalling him. "Don't you have a rule about me talking? Or that I'm not allowed to look you in the eyes? And what about safe words?"

He laughed. When he laughed like that, Mr. Sutton had a face to behold. His mouth, his cheeks, his eyes, his handsome face became…extraordinary. If Helen of Troy launched a thousand ships, Mr. Sutton would launch an entire air force when he laughed.

"You can say whatever you want. The more you fight, the better I like it." He raised a brow wickedly. "Because then you'll get punished."

"Punished how?"

He shook his head. "I'll describe it when you have your clothes off." That sounded ominous. "And you can look at me all you like." He stepped closer, so close she could smell his male heat. "I want to see your eyes on me when my cock is in your mouth," he whispered against her hair.

She was *so* wet. This was what she wanted, the heat, the need, the desire.

He stepped back, looked at her peaked nipples against the camisole, her flushed skin. "So tell me, do you really need a safe word? Is there anything I want that you won't do for me?"

Nothing. Absolutely nothing. Although... "I have to admit that when I was picking out those gags you wanted, I preferred the O-ring over the spider gag. *That* was scary." One was a simple ring that held the mouth open, and she'd felt a dirty little thrill. The other looked like some sort of dental dam that stretched your lips and hooked into your mouth...and...well...no. No way.

He laughed again, then relaxed into a smile. "This is going to be fun, Miss Dawson. I will take that under advisement. O-ring okay, spider gag no go. If you prove trustworthy and do what I say, I might consider granting that wish." He shook his finger. "But if you cross me, I'll know just what to use on you."

Damn. She shouldn't have said a word about the spider gag.

"Now take off the rest of your clothing. I'm perfectly aware you're stalling." He stepped behind her, popped the top button, and unzipped her skirt. With a little push, the material pooled around her high heels. With him unable to see her full frontal view, she whisked the camisole over her head and tossed it. Her breasts bounced. She stood with her eyes closed a moment, feeling the brush of the overhead air across her skin and the heat of his gaze on her backside.

"Pantyhose are out, Miss Dawson." She felt him circle her. "Take them off now." He leaned in. "I want your bare necessities accessible to me at all times." He tipped her chin. "Look at me." The pad of his finger was slightly rough on her chin, his pale blue eyes taken over by his pupils. "Don't close your eyes again. You need to see everything I'm going to do to you." The whispered words were a hard command.

Stepping back, he waggled a finger at her. "The pantyhose. I want them gone. You really must learn to react immediately when I issue a command, Miss Dawson. Or it will involve punishment."

"Yes sir." She kicked aside her skirt, stepped out of her shoes, then stuck her thumbs in the waistband of her hose and rolled them down. She'd shaved her legs and smoothed on mango body lotion. The fruity scent rose to her nostrils along with the aroma of her desire. She could actually smell how wet she was.

"Now put the shoes back on."

She now stood before him clad only in her panties. Her skin was hot beneath his perusal, a mixture of arousal, embarrassment, and fear. What if he didn't like what he saw? The women with whom he was photographed were gym-toned, pampered, and prepped.

He trailed his fingers along the underside of her breast, then slid across to circle her nipple. Monica couldn't suppress a delicious shiver.

"Your nipples are tight little pearls begging for my touch," he murmured, all his concentration on the small bud beneath his fingers. Then he pinched her.

She cried out with shock and nerves as a jolt of sensation streaked straight down to her center, the pleasure and pain all rolled together into a potent mixture. Warmth gushed between her legs, and a need she'd never known weakened her knees.

"Did it hurt?"

She couldn't catch her breath so all she did was nod.

"Did you like it?"

She nodded again, her skin hot, her limbs trembling for him.

"Good. Pleasure and pain come from the same knife, just different edges of it. They work best when applied together."

"Yes sir," she whispered.

He laughed. "You've been reading too much. I'm Mr. Sutton to you, the way I've always been. No *sir*, no *master*."

She'd actually been looking forward to calling him Master.

"Panties. Off. I want you naked, Miss Dawson." He narrowed his eyes, dropped his voice dangerously. "And I want it now."

She slipped her bikini panties over her hips. Moist with her desire, they clung to her apex a moment. Then she slid them down her legs.

"Give them to me," Mr. Sutton demanded. When she handed them over, he put the fragrant material to his nose and breathed her in.

It was the most erotic moment she'd ever experienced, his lids at half mast, lips curved, a look of pure bliss on his arrogant features. All her fears about rejection, her body, and his approval simply melted away beneath that look.

He buried her panties in his suit pocket. "You're very wet, Miss Dawson."

"Yes." She was faint with desire. She stood naked before a man, before the windows, before the world. She would have done anything he asked, right there, for anyone to see.

"Do you want my cock, Miss Dawson?" He unbuttoned the jacket revealing the hard ridge of his erection.

She'd dreamed of putting her mouth on him, and she salivated. If she'd had more voice in that moment, she'd have begged, but all she could manage was a croaked "Yes."

"Good." The suit fell closed again. "You're not ready for it yet."

She wanted to weep with need. She wanted to shout that

she was more than ready. She would show him how good she was, how good she could make him feel.

He circled her again, whispering to her. "No, Miss Dawson, you're not ready," he repeated as if she'd said all that aloud.

"You need to be disciplined. You need to be trained." His voice was all around her. "You need to earn the first taste of my cock. You need to show obedience. And you need to be punished when you don't obey."

"I will obey." If her voice had been louder, the tone would have been strident.

"You *say* you will, but you've demonstrated far too much willfulness today. Asking too many questions. Taking too long to execute my commands." His voice was a low drawl, soft, almost gentle. Until he added quickly, harshly, "Have you ever been spanked, Miss Dawson?"

"No."

He continued to circle her slowly, taking stock of her, his gaze touching her, yet he never put his hands on her. "You will be spanked. Sometimes as a punishment, and sometimes simply because I take pleasure in it. You will need to be gagged when you talk too much. You will need to be restrained. And"—behind her, his breath caressed her nape—"you will need to be flogged."

Monica swallowed hard. He'd once had her purchase a flogger, his instructions very explicit on exactly what he wanted her to buy. The spider gag had jangled nerves her more than the flogger, but still...

"I won't be bad. I won't need to be flogged."

"Sometimes you will need it," he insisted against the knot of hair against her neck , his closeness, his heat, his testosterone making her a little crazy. She wanted to pull the pins from her bun and entice him as her hair fell free. "Sometimes I'll simply want to take my flogger to your backside."

She shivered.

"Slap, slap, slap," he chanted. "Against your ass. And

your most private parts." He dropped his voice to a hiss. "Against your sweet, delectable pussy."

There was fear. There was desire. And then there was the wild need to feel exactly what he described. She'd never thought about bondage or submission or pain until she'd come to work for him. Then she couldn't stop wondering how anyone could find pleasure in pain, couldn't stop imagining how the devices he had her buy would make her feel. It had become an obsession to find out. *He* had become her obsession.

"So you're saying I don't even have to do anything wrong in order to be punished?"

He chuckled. She shuddered. And closed her eyes briefly before he stopped his pacing right in front of her. "I will teach you to want it, need it. You'll beg for it." He held her gaze. "And you'll love it." He trailed a finger straight down between her breasts, ending just above her pubic line. "Just like you love standing naked in front of me. You're already used to that, aren't you?"

She had been until he brought it up. She flushed with embarrassment again. "Not really."

He laughed. And she melted for him again. "You will do so many things for me that you've never considered doing. After work, I want you to stop by our usual establishment and purchase a vibrator. Charge it to my account."

She blinked. "Buy it for who?"

He smiled indulgently at her. "For you."

"I thought doms didn't let their submissives have orgasms unless they gave permission."

Closing his eyes, he shook his head as if she'd severely saddened him. Or disgusted him. "I don't care what you've read on the Internet. You will be required to give yourself multiple orgasms several times a day." He raised his brows at her. "The more a woman comes, the more she needs to come. I want you thinking about sex all the time." Her skin heated as he spoke. "I want you begging for it, dying for it." Then he chucked her under the chin. "You just can't let anyone *else* make you come unless I grant permission."

"Oh." A vibrator. Multiple orgasms a day. She wanted to beg for one now. From him. She didn't want another man to make her climax.

"Now get dressed, Miss Dawson. We don't want to miss that conference call with Petarie."

Conference call? Petarie? It took her a moment to remember. It took her a moment to even recall her first name.

As she dressed, Mr. Sutton bent down and snatched her pantyhose from the carpet. "We'll trash these." Then he patted his pocket. "And I'll keep your panties."

Oh God. He expected her to walk around without her panties or hose for the rest of the day. She'd be completely naked under her skirt. Her face flushed. "Don't we need some sort of contract?"

He laughed again. "You really do read too much. We don't need a contract. We only have one rule, remember?"

"Yes. But…" How did she say it so it didn't sound like begging? "I'm not sure about the duration of our arrangement."

"Ah, the length of time. Yes." He rounded his desk, grabbed a sheet of paper out of his printer, and slapped it down on a folder. "Here's the rule." He wrote with a flourish. "And let's review our arrangement in two months." Another flourish. He twisted the note on the desk to face her. "Feel better with it all written down?"

She wasn't sure. In two months, he could beg her to stay. Or he could fire her because nothing had worked. Yet she'd done this to herself. "Yes."

"Then sign."

She signed and dated on the line he'd drawn below his signature.

Snatching their contract back, he filed it in his drawer. "Now. The conference call."

Just as she reached the door, he said, "We'll need to go shopping for your new lingerie. I want you in thigh-high stockings. So much more accessibility, don't you think?"

She felt her cheeks blush, both sets.

"And remember when you're picking out your new vibrator that everything you buy from now on will be used on you."

She almost tripped. Honestly, what had she gotten herself into?

CHAPTER THREE

Rance fished her panties from his pocket, pink no-frills bikinis. They were still warm with her heat and damp with her dew. He steeped himself in her scent again.

He wanted this. He wanted *her*. He felt alive again, his skin buzzing, every sense on alert. His fingers still retained the tactile memory of her skin against them.

Miss Dawson had appeared a bit shell-shocked as she left his office. She was perfect. In the space of an hour, she'd hooked him with her naiveté and her desire. She'd agreed to follow his every instruction, do anything he asked. And he was already making plans for her.

After it was all over, though, they wouldn't be able to return to the seamless working relationship they'd had. He felt a little wistfully sad for its demise, and also for the eventual demise of this new relationship they'd started. Because of course it was lust and would therefore end. He'd learned the hard way that love, at least romantic love, was dreamed up by poets.

He'd married his first wife for love. He'd been young, idealistic. And stupid. He'd worked hard, climbing the corporate ladder. She'd complained bitterly about his long hours, but she complained even harder when he suggested he take a job with less hours, which would also mean less pay. So he continued to climb. Until he scavenged a half day off to take her to the beach for her birthday. Unfortunately, she was already celebrating. In their bed. With another man. It was the fact that he'd been more angry than hurt that made him aware of the nonexistence of love.

The second time, he'd married for convenience. He needed a hostess and a companion. His chosen candidate needed his money and his social standing. A match made in heaven. Until he discovered that she was using the monthly allowance he provided her with to pay for an apartment where she met her lover.

He was a cuckold twice over. And he hadn't even gotten to enjoy it. Not like he did now, where he chose the men with whom his submissives had sex. While he watched. Or participated. Or did whatever the hell he wanted. When his submissives were as disobedient as his wives had been, he punished them. It had worked very well. Until the boredom set in. Which was also about the time he realized his women had all become too much like his ex-wives.

Then this morning his Miss Dawson—his Monica—had put her resume on his desk. She'd removed her clothes for him. She'd looked close to orgasm when he tweaked her nipple. And his cock had been harder than he remembered it being in months, maybe years.

Oh yes, he had very big plans for her.

⊙≪≫

"He sent you out to buy a vibrator?" Sean stood in the doorway of her bathroom as Monica leaned over the pedestal sink to remove her makeup. The cube-size room with its tiled floor was large enough for the claw foot tub, a sink, toilet, and the small vanity.

"It's not like he hasn't sent me out for stuff like that before." She sounded slightly defensive.

"Yes. But not for *you*." He sounded aghast that she

couldn't understand the difference.

And she didn't. In fact, the other shopping expeditions were worse, at least in the beginning. Now, however, she'd visited the exclusive shop so many times, it no longer embarrassed her. They even knew her name, and Mr. Sutton had an account. Thank goodness he wasn't running for political office or the press would have a field day with that.

"Would you quit pestering me with questions? This is private." It had been a momentous day, and she needed a little peace in her own bathroom.

"Sweetie, we don't keep anything private," he drawled.

That was true. He came in to sit on the closed toilet lid. She was dressed only in bra and panties. It still gave her a thrill that Mr. Sutton had kept the bikinis she'd worn this morning.

"You don't have any girlfriends," Sean went on. "So you have to tell *me* everything."

Sean *was* her girlfriend. Because he was potential competition for the same men, women didn't like having him around. What if—God forbid—a man her female friend was interested in actually chose Sean? And the men Monica dated didn't like him because he was potential competition for her. Even though he was gay. It didn't make a lot of sense. Sean was also quite outspoken. He said what he thought and everyone's feelings be damned. He believed most people were in denial and it was his duty to tell them the truth.

For the most part, he was right, but that didn't always endear him to people.

When Monica didn't want the truth, she simply edited the details she revealed. Like she did now. She didn't tell him Mr. Sutton had ordered her to take off her clothes. She didn't say she'd been wet and ready to come. She hadn't said a thing about the daily multiple orgasms. Though she'd had to appease Sean by telling him *something*, and since she'd come home with the vibrator—which he'd seen when he followed her into the bedroom—it was the logical choice.

"So what are you supposed to do with it?" Sean wanted the prurient details.

She wasn't about to give them so she simply gave him the evil eye in the mirror.

"You know you want to share," he cajoled.

She wasn't sure. She was still in upheaval. She'd gotten naked for her boss, let him pinch her nipple, and steal her panties. Then...nothing. They'd worked as if the whole episode in his office hadn't happened. She set up the conference call, went through the mail, returned voice messages, booked the Chicago trip—ugh, Chicago in August—answered Mr. Sutton's emails or marked the ones he needed to look at himself, ordered supplies, and on and on. Then after work, she'd bought a vibrator.

"He didn't tell me what I'm supposed to use it for." Not in specific words.

"But you put it in your briefcase, so he wants it for something."

She shot him the eye again. "Do you need to watch every move I make?"

He grinned. "What are friends for? So tell me more."

What *more* could she give him without giving away everything? She sighed. "He's going to take me shopping for lingerie."

"Get out," Sean crowed. He punched the air. "You got naked for him."

Damn. It wasn't the right thing to reveal. "What does buying lingerie have to do with getting naked for him?"

"How else would he know your lingerie selection is so blah?"

"Gee, thanks."

"I mean it in the nicest possible way."

"How can that be nice?"

He shook his head. "Just be sure you get a lot of really nice stuff, some jewelry, too. Because once it's over, you'll be looking for another job. So make the most of it now."

She pursed her lips as she smoothed on night cream.

"You don't know what'll happen."

"Please." He rolled his eyes. "We both know what happens to women who screw the boss."

"I'm not screwing him. I'm becoming his submissive."

Sean stared her down in the mirror. "And there's a difference?"

"Of course there is." She grabbed her robe off the back of the door and tugged it on. As if being in her skivvies in front of Sean suddenly revealed too much. Crossing her arms, she gave him her full attention. "I want to try this, Sean. I've thought about it for a long time. You know that. And if I have to find a new job, then I have to find a new job. But I'm taking this risk. I want to explore. I want to find out what this whole BDSM thing he does is all about." And she wanted only Mr. Sutton to teach her. "You always tell me I don't take risks, so at least support me when I finally do it."

He rose, put his arm around her, and shoved her head down on his shoulder. "I support you. I just hate it when you get hurt. I figure that if I prepare you ahead of time, you won't feel so bad because you're expecting it."

Sean had a wonderful way of *preparing* her. When she dated a man he didn't like—which was most of the time— he made sure she was aware of every single flaw. And he was right, because after the glow of the first few weeks or months wore off, those flaws started to grate on her nerves. When the relationship ended, Sean was there to pick up the pieces.

Mr. Sutton was different. She stepped back to look at Sean. "Please don't do it this time. I won't be able to share anything with you if you do. I don't want you pick-pick-picking."

"Aw, baby, I'm sorry. You know I love you. I just want what's best for you. But I don't trust him. He'll grind you down until there's nothing left."

"You're doing it again," she singsonged at him.

He raised his hands in surrender. "All right. I won't say

another word." He zipped his lips. "But you have to share every dirty detail. Deal?"

"Only if you share every dirty detail about Jim." To be completely honest, the dirty details of Sean's sex life aroused her. Especially when he tried taboo stuff at work. The pursuit of Jim, who pretended disinterest but always seemed to show up in out-of-the-way places where Sean could put his hands on him, was exciting.

"Deal," Sean agreed, with a naughty twinkle in his eye.

She wondered if she was making a bargain with the devil. Make that two bargains with two devils in one day.

⁓

There had been more expensive vibrators, with multiple speeds, rotating beads, and protrusions designed to stimulate inside and out. Monica had chosen a simple model where all she had to do was twist the base to turn it on and increase the speed. Of course, she had a vibrator in her bedside drawer, but he'd demanded she buy a new one, and she'd purchased something similar to what worked for her at home.

She arrived before Mr. Sutton the next morning, the device stowed in her briefcase and still in its packaging. Her desk didn't have the opulence of his, but at least it was wood rather than steel. No Persian rugs either, just basic wall-to-wall carpet in a pretty shade of durable blue. Her computer was state of the art and her chair ergonomic. The filing cabinets were oak and the visitor chairs along the wall were comfortable. For reading material on the side table, she'd chosen financial magazines like *Fortune, Forbes,* and *The Economist.* A smaller flat-panel TV than the one in Mr. Sutton's office, also tuned to *Bloomberg,* was strategically mounted on the wall. Not that anyone used the chairs or read the magazines or watched the ticker tape scroll on *Bloomberg* because Mr. Sutton rarely kept anyone waiting. Monica worked with the sound muted on the television.

The coffee maker and condiments were on the wet bar in the conference room, along with a small set-in fridge. Monica brown-bagged, and the special coffee she purchased for Mr. Sutton needed to be refrigerated as well. The cabinet above the wet bar housed a selection of liquor and wines. They were not a corporation with a policy manual, and if Mr. Sutton wished to serve his guests wine or something a little stronger, he did.

The coffee finished brewing, and Monica was pouring herself a cup just as Mr. Sutton arrived. She made him a cup, too. She liked cinnamon-flavored creamer, while he preferred black.

"Good morning, Miss Dawson," he said as she entered his office with the mug. "Thank you." He was always polite, and this morning he looked exceptional in a gray pin-striped suit.

"You're welcome." She was also polite. In fact, they were too damn polite after what had occurred yesterday. "No appointments this morning, but you've got lunch with Erin and Dominic DeKnight. They're the couple looking for an expansion investment. And you meet with Mr. Jones in the conference room at three."

"What's tomorrow look like?"

He could access his schedule as easily as she could but giving him a rundown was part of their routine. "Your usual Friday breakfast with your mother. Connor Kingston for lunch. No afternoon appointments."

"Thank you, Miss Dawson."

He let her walk out of his office without a word about the vibrator or the fact that her legs were bare. No pantyhose, just as he'd instructed. Dammit, didn't he even notice?

She couldn't concentrate on emails or listing the opening stock quotes for him. All she could think about was the vibrator in her briefcase. She transferred it from the case to the bottom desk drawer, stared at the plastic package, glanced at his open office door. His phone line was lit. Who was he talking to? Since his desk was on the far side of the office, his voice was nothing more than a low murmur.

She realized she'd had her hands poised over the keyboard for several long moments without typing a thing.

His phone light went out. Monica started typing, but she actually had her fingers on the wrong key set and everything came out gobbledygook.

The intercom buzzed before his voice came through. "Are you alone, Miss Dawson?"

Of course she was. He knew that. She tapped the button. "Yes, Mr. Sutton."

"Then lock the outer door and come into my office. Bring your purchase."

Her blood began to rush through her veins. Yes. Just what she'd been waiting for. She left the gobbledygook on her screen and jumped to do his bidding.

It couldn't have been more than fifteen seconds before she entered his inner sanctum. The TV screen over the mantel was off, and Mr. Sutton sat on the sofa, his legs crossed.

"Stand by the fireplace," he ordered. He'd removed his suit jacket. His shirt was crisply white and his blue-and-gray striped tie firmly in place. "Let me see what you bought."

Once in position, she held out her purchase.

"It's still in the plastic," he said, frowning.

Her pulse skipped at his harsh tone. "Yes…well…"

"Did I not specifically tell you that you needed several climaxes a day in order to create your orgasmic addiction?"

She wanted to laugh, but he sounded absolutely serious, with not a single decipherable expression on his features. "I don't recall you mentioning orgasmic addiction, Mr. Sutton."

"I told you," he emphasized, "that the more a woman climaxes, the more she *needs* to climax." He tapped his temple. "Was I speaking to myself? Or maybe I was alone in the room?"

He was teasing her. He must be. Wasn't he? "No, I was

there. I just didn't realize you meant I was supposed to go home and use the vibrator." She'd thought he was going to use it on her himself. Today. Right now.

"I didn't hire you as my submissive because you're stupid. In future, you will learn to interpret my meaning correctly. Now open the package."

"Yes, Mr. Sutton." Maybe he was just showing her what discipline meant, that she had to anticipate what he would want even if he didn't explicitly state it. She tore at the plastic. It didn't budge. She tried sliding her thumbnail between the two edges. They were sealed tight.

He rolled his eyes heavenward, shook his head, then reached into his pants pocket and pulled out a penknife. "Hand it over. You'll probably cut yourself."

His lip quivered slightly. He was trying not to laugh. She was sure of it.

In seconds, he'd cut through the hard plastic and freed the vibrator. Holding it up, he perused her purchase. "Not bad. Easy to use."

Unscrewing the bottom, he slid in the batteries which, thankfully, had been included. Otherwise she probably would have forgotten them. Then she'd really need punishment. Monica kept the smile to herself.

When he turned it on, the thing hummed in his hand. "This will do nicely." He twisted the base to turn it off. "You appear to like no frills, Miss Dawson."

She wasn't sure what he meant by that. "It was your account. I didn't want to get extravagant."

"So solicitous, always looking out for my money."

She did his online bill-paying, and she always questioned strange charges or extraneous fees. "That's my job."

He smiled. "And now it's your job to take off your clothes. But keep the shoes." He warmed the cool plastic of the vibrator between his hands.

She didn't feel the same flush of embarrassment or nerves that she had yesterday, just the erotic thrill. She'd put her hair up in its usual knot and wore her normal style of work blouse and classic skirt, this time combining pink and navy blue. She'd donned her best bra and panties. Unfortunately no one would call them sexy. But she was aware of Mr. Sutton's avid gaze as she stripped down.

"Very good. No unpalatable pantyhose today. I'm proud of you for following at least that instruction. And for not hesitating even a second when I told you to get naked for me."

There was something sexy and a little bit dirty in the terminology. Monica's skin heated. "I'm very trainable." Except that the longer she stood naked, the more nervous she became. There was something about being the naked one in the room that made her edgy. When was he going to take off his clothes?

"Panties and bra."

Now *that* was naked naked. After Sean had left her bathroom—there were some things he didn't get to watch her do—she'd trimmed between the legs. Reaching behind, she unclasped her bra, then leaned forward to let it fall down her arms. At the same time, she slid her panties down. Rolling back up, she tried to stand straight but couldn't meet his eyes.

Until yesterday, she'd never stood naked for a man's examination.

"Very nice, Miss Dawson. I like a nice trimmed thatch. Legs apart."

She was wet and yet her skin had chilled. She planted her high heels six inches wider.

"More," he insisted.

She spread herself for him. He was up and standing behind her in three swift moves. Oh God, this was it. He was going to use the vibrator on her. Monica wanted to lay her head back on his shoulder and give in to the sharp need.

Instead, he pulled the pins from her hair and dropped them on the floor. The locks cascaded like silk over her shoulders. "You need to look like a wanton for this," he murmured. "Another time, I'll want you prim and proper.

Mostly likely in front of an audience."

Was that a threat or a promise? His hot body against hers chased away the chill. As long as he wasn't staring at her, evaluating and assessing, the idea of being watched was heady.

"Now get in the chair," he said against her hair. "Spread your legs. And demonstrate how well you can climax."

CHAPTER FOUR

Monica gasped. "What?" She hadn't meant that she wanted him to watch her *now*.

"What I say exactly when I say," Mr. Sutton reminded her. He molded her suddenly numb fingers around the vibrator. It was warm from his grip.

Her nerves were jittering as he pushed her toward the wingchair. She slid down onto the plush seat. He wanted her to do this by herself?

"I want to see everything." He returned to his place on the sofa, slung an arm along the back, crossed his legs, and settled in for the show he'd requested. "How pink you are. How wet you are. How long it takes to excite yourself. How hard you come."

His words seduced her to wetness.

"Has anyone ever watched you?" he asked.

"No." Touching yourself was a solo sport.

"What a pity. Watching a woman make herself come is intoxicating." He raised one brow. "Don't keep me waiting."

She glanced at the full bank of windows, her heart hammering.

"Let them watch. If they can."

This was what she'd signed on for. He would push her, expose her, test her. And punish her if she didn't perform. "Can I take my punishment instead?"

He gave a throaty laugh. "I can punish you, but it won't get you out of masturbating for me. I will have what I want, Miss Dawson. And right now, I want to see you with your head thrown back, your mouth open, and coming so hard you scream."

"I come very quietly."

"Not anymore." He leaned forward, lowered his voice. "When you see how hard my cock becomes, you won't be able to hold back."

God, yes, she wanted to make him hard.

She spread herself for him, looping one leg over the chair arm. Putting her head back, she closed her eyes, wet her lips, and twisted the base of the vibrator to turn it on.

"Look at me," he demanded. "But do it like you're all alone. Like you have no inhibitions. No one can see. No one can hear. And you want to scream."

How was she supposed to pretend she was alone if he made her look at him? The vibrator hummed, and she placed the edge on her clitoris. Her body jerked, then she settled. Do it like she always did it. As if she were alone. She didn't scream because of Sean being in the next room, but she wasn't going to mention Sean to Mr. Sutton.

Do it like she always did.

She put a hand down to part herself for better access and slid the vibrator down to moisten the tip. She was wet, oh yes.

Mr. Sutton's gazed focused on her cleft and the buzzing vibrator. His chest expanded with slightly more rapid breaths. His eyes darkened. He shifted, as if to accommodate a growing erection.

She slicked her tongue across her lips and angled the vibrator, rolling it around the sensitive tissues, but not going directly to her clitoris. Nice. Good. He liked it, she could tell by the new tension along his shoulders and the widening of his nostrils as he breathed deeply.

Oh yes. She closed her eyes briefly, arching into her mechanical lover. Moaning. This wasn't the way she always did it. This was better. The build wasn't as sharp, but prolonging the act made the sensations more acute.

He didn't touch himself. God, she wanted to see his hands on the rock hard bulge in his pants more than anything. She groaned. He sucked in a harsh breath as if her sounds affected him. Then inspiration struck.

She arched. "Oh that's so good, Mr. Sutton. Yes, yes." She panted, writhed on the chair, rotated her hips against the vibrator. "Do you like this, Mr. Sutton? It makes you hard, I know it does. You want to touch yourself, too." She gave a low throaty moan, bit her lip, thrust her hips up. Then she tweaked her nipple hard, the way he'd done yesterday. Electricity jolted through her. She couldn't keep her eyes open any longer, couldn't concentrate on his face. Her moves were sinuous, sensuous. She was so wet, so hot, burning up. "Oh Mr. Sutton, I want your cock in me. Fuck me, Mr. Sutton, please, please."

The words weren't for him anymore. They were what she said in her mind as she used her vibrator at night, imagining it was him. She rocked, moaned, gasped.

The orgasm swelled inside her. A wave. A tsunami. Hurricane Sutton.

Then she thrust the vibrator deep. Took herself with it. Her blood was so high that some part of her actually believed it was him. She used her finger on her clitoris at the same time, and her entire body seemed to fly apart.

She screamed for him as she climaxed.

⌖

Christ. His eyes felt like they were bulging. Everything was bulging. He literally ached, his cock throbbing. She was pink and sweet and wet. He wanted to taste her on his tongue. Bury his face in her pussy. Lick her. Drink her come.

The pounding of the vibrator mesmerized him. Monica was the definition of *abandon*. He hadn't truly believed she was capable of it. Yet she fucked herself as if she were alone. As if she were in her own bed dreaming of him, begging a figment to fuck her. The things she'd said had nearly broken his restraint.

Her cry was a long, keening wail, her body shaking, arching, flailing. The sharp, sweet scent of her climax was etched on his olfactory senses. He would close his eyes in the middle of the night and steep his mind in the remembered aroma. He'd be instantly hard and aching. No woman had ever come like that for him. Not without his help.

He was damn near driven to wrap his hand around his cock and lose himself right along with her. His balls ached for release.

But he was stronger than that. He didn't move a muscle, simply played out the climax with her, watching, breathing, needing, dying a little. Until she subsided in the chair, boneless, her head lolling to one side. The vibrator dropped from her limp fingers. She was so overcome that she didn't even move her leg from the arm of the chair.

Then he clapped.

Instead of startling the way he'd thought she would, she merely cracked one eye open. Her luscious lips curved in a sexy, wanton smile. "Why, thank you, Mr. Sutton."

"Your performance meets with my complete approval."

"Performance?" She pulled her leg in, hitching her knee up, and covering the delectable view of her sweet, moist, deliciously hot pussy. "I wasn't performing, Mr. Sutton. That was very real." She stretched, hummed, wriggled, then looked at him. "May I get dressed now?"

After you suck my cock.

He kept the words to himself. He was in control. He didn't beg. But God, she was absolutely perfect. He felt alive, energized. Potent. "Yes, you may." He allowed her to rise, then, as she stepped into her panties, added, "I've cancelled lunch with Kingston tomorrow. You and I are going on a shopping trip."

She faltered then, losing her balance slightly but recovering. She was not as unaffected as she would have him believe. He reached between the sofa cushions and pulled out the pink panties she'd worn yesterday. Wanting them close at hand, he'd stuffed them down there earlier.

Swinging the bikini on the end of his finger, he said, "As dainty as these are, we must outfit you properly. Thigh-high stockings, delectable thong panties, lacy bras." He stood, strolled to his desk, turned and leaned back against it, crossing his arms over his chest, the panties still dangling. "At least one corset, maybe two. We want to truss you up tight. Then, I believe, a trip to our favorite toy store." Her eyes widened. "I need a new flogger especially for you. Definitely an O-ring gag since you said you wouldn't mind one." He smiled. "And a spider gag for when you really need to be taught a lesson."

She blanched as she zipped her skirt.

A decidedly good threat. "And Miss Dawson, I meant what I said. Multiple orgasms per day. You will practice tonight. Do I make myself clear?"

She hadn't even finished buttoning her blouse when she rushed out. He let her go. As the door closed behind her, he padded across the carpet to the chair she'd sat in. He could smell her on it. Picking up the vibrator, he wafted it beneath his nose for a long tempting second. Then he ran his tongue up the slick side to the tip that had rested inside her. Eyes closed to enhance his other senses, he slid the vibrator into his mouth and sucked her juices from it.

She was so damn sweet.

Training Monica was going to be heaven. Maintaining control would be his own personal hell.

⁊⊗⊱

Mr. Sutton had made himself extremely clear. She was

supposed to masturbate before going to bed and come several times. God, what if she screamed at home like she had in his office? But no, without his watchful gaze, it wouldn't be the same.

Monica barely managed not to slam the office door behind her. Normally it was open, but she needed distance to recover herself. Her fingers trembled as she buttoned her blouse, then tucked it into her skirt. Her legs felt weak.

Multiple orgasms, lingerie, toys, and a spider gag. She should *never* have told him about that. Maybe he thought she really wanted to be gagged with one because she'd mentioned it. Reverse psychology, say you don't want it when really you do.

But she didn't. She couldn't imagine how it could be sexy.

Duh. That was the whole point. It wasn't sexy. It was humiliating. Dominance and submission was all about humiliation.

There were so many things she'd wanted from him. She'd wanted his cock in her mouth. She'd wanted him to tear the vibrator out of her hands and fuck her. She didn't use those kinds of words on a normal basis, but this wasn't normal. And God yes, she had *fucking* wanted it.

But he'd done nothing. He hadn't touched himself, let alone her.

What would it take to drive him to stroke his cock? She'd been out of herself, wild. All he'd done was watch. Maybe he didn't feel anything. Maybe he was impotent.

Yet, he'd been hard. As he leaned back against his desk, her panties swinging back and forth on his finger, his suit slacks had been stretched tight across his large erection.

Her clothing in place once again, she sat down at her desk, fingertips poised over the keyboard. He had wanted her, she knew it.

What would it take to break his control?

❧

"Get out of my bed, Sean."

Beside her, his weight sank into the mattress. "We had a deal. Dirty details. What happened with the vibrator? Because I know you took it with you this morning."

She sighed. "You go first. Tell me how you accosted poor Jim today."

He groaned. "He's playing hard to get."

"He always is. How did you get his attention? Because I know you did *something*."

"I followed him into the men's room."

"That's pretty bold. Then what?"

"When he was at the urinal, I sidled up behind him and nestled my cock right in the crack of his ass."

"You're so bad," she whispered, pushing back the bedclothes because she was getting a little hot under the covers. In more ways than one. "And?"

"I cupped his balls and held his cock for him while he took a leak."

"Ewwe. That's gross."

"It was hot as hell."

She couldn't deny the zing of excitement shooting through her.

"Then he zipped up, washed his hands, and left without looking at me. I was so hard I had to jerk off in the stall."

"What if someone had walked in?"

"That's why I thought he'd push me away. The risk of getting caught. But he didn't."

"He wants it bad," she said.

"Yeah. Totally. Your turn. Try to beat that one."

Oh, she could. "Mr. Sutton made me use the vibrator while he watched."

"Get out. That's gotta be grounds for sexual harassment."

"Not as bad as helping Jim take a leak right in the men's room where anyone could walk in on you."

"True." He buffed his nails on his bare chest in triumph. "Did you come?"

She nodded.

"You dirty little girl. Did he?"

"He didn't even touch himself."

Sean raised one brow, then gave her a wicked smile. "What's he want next?"

"We're going shopping tomorrow for lingerie. And toys."

"Sex toys?"

"Of course." Then she delivered the coup de grace. "And tonight I'm supposed to give myself multiple orgasms." Mr. Sutton had returned the vibrator for that express purpose.

He puffed out a breath. "Can I watch?"

"Of course not." She did, however, experience a jolt of heat at the thought. Her thighs were suddenly slippery. The idea of being watched was exciting, but it was Mr. Sutton's gaze she craved. "Besides, you're gay. You don't want to see a woman masturbate."

"It's sex, sweetie. I love sex in any form. A guy doesn't have to be gay to like watching two women kiss, right?"

"That's not the same."

"It's exactly the same. Go ahead, tell me you're not hot and bothered thinking about me and Jim in the men's room. You'll probably use it as a sex fantasy to get yourself off."

"Don't be disgusting." She didn't put any heart in the words. He was right. His tales usually made her wet. Just once she'd like to watch two men together. Or maybe twice. To satisfy her curiosity. "But you still can't watch me." It was bad enough letting Mr. Sutton watch. Though that had been extremely good. "Now go to your own room or my master will punish me if I have to report back that I didn't have my multiple orgasms."

"Spoilsport."

CHAPTER FIVE

Mr. Sutton would be late this morning since he had his weekly breakfast with his mother. He took exceptional care of her, installing her in an exclusive retirement home down on the Peninsula in Belmont. She lived in her own apartment, but took her meals in a communal dining room which served excellent food. Despite being eighty-eight years old, she walked regularly and was only slightly forgetful. Mr. Sutton visited on Fridays, and his sister stopped by to see their mother on Tuesdays. Monica doubted most families were as attentive. She was an only child, and she'd lost her parents to cancer within a couple of years of each other. If they were still alive, she wasn't sure she would have been as dutiful as the Suttons.

All that free time waiting for her boss to arrive gave her too much opportunity to think about last night. Mr. Sutton was right. Those multiple orgasms, along with Sean's encounter in the men's room, had primed her pump, so to speak. The more she thought about sex, the more she craved it. She was starving for it now.

The outer door opened. Her first sight of Mr. Sutton made her shiver. His navy blue suit accentuated his physique. Her mouth went dry as he stood tall and delicious before her desk.

"How many orgasms did you have last night?"

Well, good morning to you, too. She knew better than to say that aloud. "I think it was three."

"You *think*? How can you not *know*?" He glowered.

One orgasm just seemed to flow into another. She'd been remembering Mr. Sutton's gaze on her yesterday. That made her incredibly wet. Then there was that talk with Sean. The thing he'd done to Jim in the men's room. She couldn't help imagining it. By all rights, the story should have embarrassed her, but she and Sean could say anything to each other. They talked about sex all the time. It probably wasn't normal for heterosexual men and women, but Sean was like her best girlfriend. Except that when he talked about sex, she got aroused.

What would Mr. Sutton make of that? She'd never told him she lived with a man. Most people wouldn't understand. Besides, it wasn't his business. For some reason, though, whenever he sent a car to pick her up, whether he was in it or not, she always made sure to be downstairs waiting.

So bringing Sean up now might be a mistake. Mr. Sutton was a dom. He would be proprietary. Sean was better off remaining her secret.

She gave him half the truth. "I'm not sure exactly where one orgasm began and the other ended."

"Is that usual?"

She shook her head. "It was what you made me do yesterday." And everything he would make her do in the future.

One brow went up. "So you liked being on display."

"It made me nervous. But then it made me very wet."

His nostrils flared a moment. "Good. I told Smythe to return in half an hour." Smythe was his driver. "Any messages or emails I need to deal with before we go?"

"I left a couple of slips on your desk." Unless it was a complicated issue or the caller insisted, she took a message rather than transfer anyone to his voicemail. In the age of automated phone systems with too many numbers that needed to be pressed, it made people rest easier if they knew a person was passing on the message rather than the vagaries of electronics. "And nothing on email that needs your attention," she added.

He closeted himself in his office for the next half hour. Then, on the dot, he herded her to the elevators, a hand on her elbow. Downstairs, the car waited for them at the curb, Smythe by the door, opening it for them as they exited the building. Again, Mr. Sutton held her elbow as he helped her into the car. He'd always been solicitous even before.

"Take us to the Crocker Galleria first, Smythe."

"Yes, sir." The door closed them in.

Mr. Sutton always used the same car service and the same driver. Though he owned a BMW, he drove it only casually. For business, it was always the service. Smythe, a tall, beefy man in his thirties who could easily double as a bodyguard, didn't have a British accent despite his name. While driving, Smythe wore earbuds constantly in order to give his clients privacy. Mr. Sutton could make his business calls without being overhead.

The Crocker Galleria was an indoor mall on Post Street and only a short drive from their office building on Market. She often walked there during a Thursday lunch hour for the weekly farmer's market. The fresh vegetables and fish were to die for. Mr. Sutton had her so worked up that she'd forgotten about the market yesterday.

She didn't ask which shop they were going to, and Mr. Sutton didn't offer. Instead, he was checking his iPhone.

When they arrived at the mall, Smythe leaped out of the front seat to open the door. "When would you like me to return, sir?"

Mr. Sutton consulted his watch. "We'll need an hour."

"Very good, sir."

An hour? To buy lingerie? She knew what she liked and always got the same brand so she didn't have to try anything on. Hmm. Maybe that was why he said she needed something new.

They descended into the mall beneath the arched glass ceiling. That, along with the magnificent clock set high in the glass on one end, were what made the Crocker Galleria unique. When the sky poured with rain, the spectacle was amazing.

He led her to an exclusive and no doubt expensive lingerie shop. They were the only customers, which was probably why they were immediately set upon by a sales lady, midthirties, pretty, large breasts, and very red lips.

"How may I help you?" She spoke to Mr. Sutton as if she could tell he ruled everything. Or as if Monica was of no interest.

"We'll need several complete sets. Brassieres, panties— I prefer thongs—and stockings."

Monica wanted to giggle. It sounded as if the thongs and stockings were for him.

The sales woman merely gave him a knowing smile. "Garter belt?"

"That won't be necessary. I prefer thigh-highs."

It was a little harder to stifle the giggle. She imagined him in stockings and a thong.

"Shall we measure?" the woman queried, one hand splayed out toward Monica, the other on Mr. Sutton's arm. Her red lips seemed to pucker.

"I'm fine. I know my size." Monica realized her voice was too sharp.

"She needs to be measured," Mr. Sutton said, as if she hadn't spoken.

The sales lady ushered her away. "Please remove your blouse and skirt," the woman said once they were in the dressing room. There were mirrors all around for a three-sixty view.

She was getting used to dropping her clothes. The woman measured her hips and bustline, then wrote the information on a small card she handed to Monica. "Let me just ask what your," she paused, "*friend* would like you to try on."

She was about to say he was her boss, not her friend, but decided against it. She didn't like the woman's condescending tone. "I'll choose for myself."

The sales lady flapped a hand. "I'm sure he has some specific things in mind."

Monica stepped into her skirt. She didn't want Mr. Sutton fingering lingerie with this woman beside him, her too red lips whispering in his ear.

"Suit yourself," the woman said snidely as she pushed the curtain aside, preceding Monica. Her tone changed immediately when they returned to Mr. Sutton. "Do you have a preference on color, lace, demi cup?" She picked up a pretty white bra with a black lace overlay and held it across her chest to demonstrate the fit. "This is lovely."

Sure that the wench meant the whole package, including her breasts and those lips, Monica took Mr. Sutton's arm proprietarily. "He doesn't like white."

His tipped his head from her to the sales lady and back, as if he were watching a tennis match. Or mud wrestling. Then he smiled. "You're so right, my dear. I want black. I want red. I want extremely low cups to reveal as much creamy skin as possible. We do want to show off those beauties of yours to our audience, don't we?" He turned to the sales girl. "She's an exhibitionist, and I'm a voyeur."

The woman's lips puckered into round O of astonishment. She held the pose for a long moment, until the front door whooshed opened. Then she gasped. "My goodness, another customer. Please excuse me." She probably wouldn't be back.

"That was terrible," Monica said. But she giggled. Because she'd won. He'd chosen her.

"What?" He feigned misunderstanding with a wave of his hand. "I like the white with black lace. Here's a matching thong with lace in the strategic place." He held up the delicate panty.

Monica looked at the price tag. "Oh my God."

Mr. Sutton did not look. "I will have you dressed as I wish. Money is no object."

She'd received gifts before. Lingerie, most definitely. But this was different. This was...ownership. And it felt good.

"I want to see you in this bra." He pushed her toward the dressing room.

"You can't come in." She glanced at the sales lady who was giving them a nervous eye as she helped a matron chose a foundation garment.

"Don't argue with me. I'll stand outside. You can pull the curtain aside when you're ready."

A flush raced along her skin. *This* was exhibitionism. She unbuttoned her blouse for the second time. The woman had measured correctly and the fit was perfect, far more comfortable than her regular brand. And it damn well should be at those prices. The lace was delicate, the white silky against her skin. The confection made her feel beautiful. Perhaps that's what expensive lingerie did for a woman.

She pushed the curtain aside a couple of inches. He was right there, his eyes on her breasts. Beneath the alluring lace, her nipples peaked.

"Pretty," he said softly and ran the tip of his finger along the edge.

She was wet. Breathless. Her heart pounding.

"Needs to be lower." He pushed the material until her nipple was visible and stroked her, his gaze locking with hers.

She grabbed a hook on the wall to steady herself.

"I could come in there," he said softly. "I could push you to your knees and force my cock in your mouth. Then I could come all over that pretty black lace."

She sucked in a breath. The edge of her vision faded, everything but his face, and she swayed closer to him.

"But we wouldn't want to shock our little sales lady."

"Yes, please, let's shock her." She was dying to taste him.

"Naughty girl," he said fondly. "You'll have to wait.

Now let me pick out other pretty things I'd like to see you in."

He snapped the curtain closed. Monica sank down onto a cushioned stool. Her face was flaming. She wanted to touch herself. She would have sucked him, swallowed him, anything he wanted. And she didn't give a damn about the woman with her red lips.

In fact, Monica would have relished demonstrating exactly who owned Mr. Sutton.

❧

She would have taken him in her mouth. Rance could smell her arousal. It had been little more than three days since her outrageous act of placing her resume on his desk. And he was hooked. How could he have missed her sensual depths in the five years she'd worked for him? Ah, but he hadn't missed them. She'd simply been too good to trifle with. Now he couldn't stop.

There were two large bags in the trunk as Smythe drove them down Market Street. Lacy brassieres, satiny thongs, and silky thigh-high stockings.

"So where are we going?" Monica sat beside him, the spicy scent of her arousal still perfuming the air.

"A shop that specializes in custom-fitted corsets. You will look magnificent." The question was whether to get an underbust or an overbust. There was something to be said for showing only a hint of nipple instead of the whole breast. Teasing. Tantalizing.

"You mean like they wore in *Gone with the Wind*?"

He laughed. "Yes. It will be tight. But you'll love it."

She gave him a deadpan expression, but her eyes twinkled. "So you've tried one on?" She was laughing at him. He liked this sassy mood on her.

"You're begging for punishment," he remonstrated.

"Of course not."

But she was. And she would have it. Precisely when he

49

was ready to give it to her.

The drive was short, and Smythe pulled up near a wide alley that fronted the small shop. He'd sent women here before, but he'd never brought a lady. With Monica, he had a mind to choose everything she wore for him.

The shop was unassuming with an eclectic assortment of hand-tooled jewelry along with inexpensive beads, handmade hats hanging on racks or perched on decorated Styrofoam heads, scarves, panties, all sorts of feminine fripperies in an assortment of antique display cases. And the corsets. His body tightened at the thought of her cinched into a boned undergarment, her breasts plumping over the top like a saucy tavern wench. He made up his mind on the style, definitely overbust.

A young woman in her late twenties entered from a back room to greet them. A jaunty gray hat topped her ponytail, matching her gray sweater and black leggings. Dark-framed glasses gave her a serious look, and the measuring tape around her neck spoke of an all-business mindset.

She turned to Monica rather than to him. "May I help you find something?"

He wanted her in no doubt as to who would be choosing. "I will be outfitting my lady with a corset. Overbust." He angled his hand at chest height to indicate what he wanted. "With the sweetheart cut rather than the straight-line." He was sure there was a special name for it, but couldn't remember.

"Have you ever worn a corset before?" she inquired, insisting on bringing Monica into the decision-making.

Monica was already stepping down into the main room, touching material swatches. "No, I haven't."

The girl followed her. "Contrary to what most people believe, they're quite comfortable when worn properly. They enhance your posture as well."

"So it's not like Mammy cinching Scarlett while she held onto the bedpost?" Monica made the *Gone with the Wind* analogy again.

The girl laughed. "The cinching is the fun part when you have the right partner." She eyed Rance knowingly. "Let's measure you."

Unlike the clerk at the lingerie shop—he didn't like pushy women—this girl was fast and efficient with her measuring tape without requiring Monica to remove her clothes. Too bad.

Then she pulled a sampler from a rack along the back wall. "Let's try this one. We can put it on over your blouse."

"No," Rance said. "I'd prefer to see the full effect without the blouse."

"That's not necessary. Many women wear camisoles underneath," she explained.

He leveled her with a look she couldn't ignore. Monica watched the byplay, a slight smile curving her lips as if she enjoyed the fact that this young one kept questioning him.

Of course, he won. As the girl ushered Monica into a tiny dressing room in the corner, he sat on the Victorian sofa, his heart beating fast with anticipation. The lingerie had gotten him hard. The corset would make him ache with need. He might very well lose a little of his control when they returned to the car. And he was looking forward to it.

CHAPTER SIX

Monica sucked in her breath.

"Start off slowly," the sales girl directed. "The more you wear it, the tighter it can be cinched over time. You might also be interested in the underbust style which, as the name implies, fits under the breasts rather than over."

The girl had given Monica a brochure of the different styles, as if making sure she knew she had choices regardless of what Mr. Sutton said. She'd almost had a heart attack when she'd seen the prices.

"One of our corsets will last you a lifetime if you take proper care of it," the girl had said quickly in explanation.

Mr. Sutton was paying for what he wanted. Price was no object.

She surveyed the corset in the mirror. It was definitely sexy. "I prefer the overbust." She wanted her breasts tempting rather than all out there.

The clerk tied off the laces, then tucked them into the top of the corset. "I'll step out to let you situate yourself. Lean forward and lift the girls up." She demonstrated before leaving.

The girls. Cute. Monica leaned forward and lifted as instructed. The corset was tight but it didn't hurt. It didn't stop deep breaths either. When she looked at herself in the mirror…oh yes, that's why women had tortured themselves with these things for centuries. Her waist was a perfect hourglass, her breasts plumped deliciously over the top. Smoothing her hands over her hips, she looked utterly gorgeous. The material was a plain red poplin with silver clasps, but she imagined herself in satin. The everyday black skirt suddenly became couture when matched with the corset. She felt sexy, wanton. As if at the snap of her fingers, she was wet, her skin flushed in the mirror.

This was the woman she wanted to be for him. A wanton creature ready for anything.

She pushed aside the curtain with a flourish.

"Beautiful," the girl said.

Mr. Sutton lounged on a sofa that was meant for dainty perching and looked fragile enough to break under his weight. A magnificent corset made of peacock feathers stood in a display case next to him. He was surrounded by colored panties, silk scarves, and sparkling beads, pretty girlie things, yet he was utterly male. The pure sexual appreciation in his gaze heated her deep inside. Her nipples were hard, almost bursting from the corset.

The look he gave her was more than worth the price of the corset. Monica preened for him, pirouetting on her high heels.

"Perfect," he said. "I want one in red satin." His voice seemed to crack on the word. "And another in white with a black lace overlay." Monica realized he was holding several material samples, fingering them, testing the feel. "When can you have them ready?"

She felt the words he didn't say, the question he didn't ask. *When can I fuck her in them? How soon? Very soon.*

It wasn't the tight corset stealing her breath. It was him, the desire scored into the lean lines of his face.

He rose, circled her like a big jungle cat. "Yes, absolutely perfect." Then he leaned close, his breath warm against her skin, his voice low. "When you go back in the dressing, take off your panties."

It would have been an order if his voice hadn't been harsh with banked need. In this moment, she was the master and he was the slave.

⌘

Monica was completely sexed up by the time they climbed into the back of the car. Dressing, undressing, the silky lingerie, the tight corset that made her aware of every curve she possessed, his light touches, his heated gaze, yes, she was wet and crazy with desire.

"I smell sex on you," he whispered.

She glanced at Smythe. He wore the earbuds and wouldn't hear a thing. His eyes were glued to the road, the rush of traffic, and the madness of pedestrians.

"Don't look at him," Mr. Sutton admonished. "Concentrate on doing what I say. Spread your legs for me."

His command sent a quiver through her. The skirt wasn't flared, and she had to hike it higher on her thighs to be able to part her knees.

His hand was immediately between her legs. Her panties were in her purse.

"Christ, you're wet."

She bit her lips, closed her eyes, held her breath. She could have come for him then, with just a little movement, the pressure of his touch. Should she beg?

"Dirty bitch. Did you touch yourself in the dressing room?"

The name excited her. She'd be a dirty bitch for him He flicked a finger across her clitoris. Her body jolted. The gasp was involuntary. "No."

"But you wanted to."

"I wanted you to do it." Her breath puffed, and she squirmed in the seat, trying to create the friction she needed.

Then her hand acted independently, totally out of her control, and she placed her palm over his between her legs.

She rocked with him, moving his hand the way she needed, and a moan fell from her lips.

He withdrew, and she heard the smack of his lips. Dammit, she shouldn't have made a sound. Opening her eyes, she watched him lick his fingers clean, tasting her desire.

"You're very sweet, my dear." Then he leaned forward, tapped Smythe on the shoulder and, when an earbud was removed, said, "Take us to the toy store."

Smythe often drove her to the shop when Mr. Sutton sent her on an errand, so he knew exactly where it was.

Mr. Sutton checked his text messages as Monica sat in the corner, her body vibrating. She couldn't turn it on and off the way he did. Perhaps that was the reason a person chose to be a dom while another submitted. It was all about who had more control. Yet in the small corset shop, she knew she'd been on top. She'd felt her control over him deep in her bones. Yet the power had been fleeting.

He laid his phone on the seat and turned, spearing her with his gaze. "I didn't tell you to touch me when I had my hand on you. You were trying to get me to give you an orgasm."

"No, I just got carried away."

"Liar," he accused mildly. "That's two infractions. I might have been able to forgive one, but a second deserves punishment."

Two? She couldn't remember the first one. "But—"

He held up a palm. "Don't make it worse."

"When?" *Now. Please.* The thought of what he would do to her made her breathless.

"When I decide."

The car glided to the curb, and Smythe got out to open the door. Mr. Sutton slid out after her. Her knees were weak, with anticipation, need, and even a little fear. *When?* Whenever he decided. *Whatever* he decided.

There was no parking on the street, and the car pulled away with a minimum of noise. The door before them was black with ornate gold trim. The shiny gold sign decorating the polished surface read *Hopkins House*. A small peephole lay beneath it. This store was exclusive. You had to be known. Entry wasn't granted to just anyone. Mr. Sutton pushed the gold button by the side of the door. Moments later, it opened.

Their hostess was in her midfifties, with cat's eye glasses like a movie spinster would wear. Her hair was sprinkled with silver, but her face was smooth and mobile. It wasn't Botox. Or any of the other cosmetic injections. It was sex, she'd once told Monica. Really good sex and often. *Sex is the elixir of life.* Of course, her good complexion might have come from very good surgery as well.

"I hope you've chosen a good selection for us to peruse, Ms. Hopkins." Mr. Sutton gestured for Monica to follow the woman up a set of wide wooden stairs that didn't creak.

Monica had always found it easier to work with Ms. Hopkins versus one of the male assistants. Asking a woman to show you a dual-headed dildo was less embarrassing than confronting a man with the question.

"We've set out several excellent samples of each of your requests," Ms. Hopkins said as she reached the top step and opened a second door leading into the shop itself.

So, Mr. Sutton had called ahead. Since he hadn't directed Monica to do it, she could only imagine the surprises—and terrors—he had in store for her.

Hopkins House was more akin to an art gallery than a sex shop. Except that the art was all sexual. Gold-trimmed antique chairs surrounded marble tables scattered in discreet corners. Vintage wood and glass cabinets displayed hand-blown glass dildos. Perfect when heated in warm water, Monica had been told. Tooled floggers, crafted leather whips, masks, blindfolds, handcuffs, and butt plugs were laid out like fine china wares. This was no sleazy sex shop where customers pawed through racks of cheap toys. Here, you described what you wanted and samples were brought from a mysterious back room. You were seated at a marble table and offered coffee and tea sandwiches while you made your selections. Shopping at Hopkins House was an event.

The carpet was plush beneath her feet as Ms. Hopkins led them to a table already festooned with assorted devices beside the tea sandwiches.

Monica was starving, it was past lunchtime, and she ate two small sandwiches to appease her hunger even as her heart went into overdrive. Her mouth dried up. There were floggers of various materials, suede, leather, even vinyl. Blindfolds in different fabrics and styles, and handcuffs, a few fur-lined, some made of leather and buckles.

She could handle all of that. It was the assortment of gags that made her quiver. She glanced at him. Mr. Sutton smiled. He'd done it on purpose, chosen the one thing she'd said she didn't want.

"Do you like them?" Mr. Sutton asked. He picked up the spider gag. "How about this one?"

"A delicious choice," their hostess intoned. "When I'm looking for something"—she puckered her lips a moment, thinking—"extraordinarily nasty, I always go for the spider gag."

The thing looked exactly like its name, a strap that went around the head with two steel hooks on either side to hold the mouth open wide. Monica wondered if Ms. Hopkins wore it herself or forced a submissive to wear it. She'd never been sure whether Ms. Hopkins was a dominatrix or a slave.

"We'll save this for extreme punishment," her magnanimous master said. "When Miss Dawson has been terribly bad."

As soon as she'd said it, she'd known it was a bad idea. Of course, he'd pick up on it. And she didn't have a safe word, for God's sake. What had she been thinking? Oh, right, she hadn't been thinking at all.

But she knew better than to argue about it now.

"What else would you recommend for Miss Dawson? I'm partial to a suede flogger." He stroked the soft material.

"That's a very good choice," Ms. Hopkins agreed, both

of them discussing Monica as if she weren't there. "It stings pleasantly but doesn't leave marks."

"Well, thank goodness I won't have marks," Monica said.

They both looked at her as if suddenly realizing she could speak. Then Ms. Hopkins smiled. "And don't forget that it's pleasant."

"I'm not really sure how getting flogged can be pleasant."

The woman put her hand on Monica's arm. "Oh my dear, you just wait. When it's done by the right dom"—she closed her eyes as if going into ecstasy—"it's excruciatingly erotic."

Despite her misgivings, her skin heated beneath the gentle stroke of Ms. Hopkins' hand. "And the gag?" Monica asked softly.

Ms. Hopkins stroked the O-ring. "Your dom has complete control over your mouth. You're at his mercy. You give up everything to him. When he inserts his cock, when you have no choice but to take him deep, he owns you." She smiled dreamily at that. "But you own him, too."

Monica felt herself entering a fantasy state, the woman's voice hypnotic. She imagined Mr. Sutton's flogger on her skin, his cock in her mouth, the gag allowing him to do anything. Except that he didn't need a gag for that. He didn't need a flogger. She'd do anything without all the trappings. She was wet, right in front of this virtual stranger, her panties damp, her nipples hard against her bra, Mr. Sutton's scent swirling around her. She felt him there, close, his body heat arcing across the space between them.

"You want that, don't you," Ms. Hopkins said in that mesmerizing tone.

"Yes," Monica said, not sure what she was agreeing to but not caring either.

"The flogger," the woman said. "The O-ring. Fur-lined leather cuffs. And a satin blindfold."

"No blindfold," Mr. Sutton said, his hand cupping

Monica's thigh possessively. "I want her to see everything I do to her. Add the spider gag in as well."

Monica shuddered.

"Perfect. I'll wrap up your purchases. Shall I put it on your account?"

"Naturally."

She was all efficiency now, that low, hypnotic quality of voice having vanished. Yet Monica still felt off balance, as if they'd seduced her together, the woman's touch, her voice, and Mr. Sutton's scent.

She was still starving, as if the constant sexual barrage had stimulated other appetites as well. She polished off the two sandwiches left on the plate. She'd probably eaten two to Mr. Sutton's every one. But what did it matter? She was crazy anyway.

With his purchases bagged, he ushered her down the stairs, the door above closing behind them. At the bottom, he pushed her against the wall.

"Lift your skirt."

She obeyed until cool air brushed across her mound. So close she could see his pupils, Mr. Sutton possessed her, his hand between her legs, caressing, teasing, testing.

"Still wet."

"Yes," she murmured. In the space of a few moments, she was ready to beg again. He'd had her on edge all day.

And still he stroked her. Monica braced herself against the wall.

"You will take the O-ring gag if I desire it."

She wet her lips. The caresses went on and on. Her legs might buckle. Oh God, she might come. She wanted to come, needed to. "Yes, Yes, I'll do it."

His mouth was a kiss away. She wanted his lips on her.

"You will never contradict me in front of anyone again."

"No." She hadn't contradicted, had she? She couldn't remember what she said. "Never."

Her body quivered, her legs quaked. Breath puffed from her throat.

He dropped to one knee in front of her and touched his tongue to her center. It was so unexpected she gasped. He sucked, licked, and she was lost, exploding from the inside out, moaning, gripping his head, holding him tight, her orgasm lightening quick after the day-long tease.

Then someone pressed the bell outside.

Rance had straightened her skirt, licked her taste from his lips, and opened the outer door. Smythe ushered them to the car he'd double-parked at the curb.

Christ. He could have taken her against the wall. He should have. His balls ached with desire. But tonight would be better, the wait keeping him on edge. And he needed that edge. One taste of her had ignited something inside him. He usually waited much longer than this before taking a taste. Hands only. Teasing only. But Monica drove him to excess. What should have been a lesson turned into an uncontrollable need. If she hadn't come on his tongue so quickly, he was sure he would have buried himself in her right up there against the wall.

Hattie Hopkins was right. A woman could own a man when his cock was in her mouth no matter the restraints he had on her. Hattie had been a handful in her day. She probably still was, but their relationship had ended years ago, not badly, just over. Oddly, it had been around the time Monica Dawson had come to work for him.

He'd enjoyed sending Monica to Hopkins House for Hattie's words of wisdom. It occurred to him that he'd been yearning for Monica all along. If not, why on earth would he send his secretary to a sex shop? Perhaps he'd been grooming her without realizing. He'd always told himself it was simply the delight he found in her shock whenever he asked for something outrageous. But perhaps it had been a test.

In the seat beside him, Monica was still dazed. It was

time to take control. "Smythe," he called out, loud enough to penetrate the earbuds. Smythe knew when to listen and when to shut out everything but the sound of his latest crime thriller in his ears.

"Yes, sir."

"We'll drive Miss Dawson home."

"Certainly, sir."

"And please return for her at eight tonight. Bring her to my flat."

"Of course, sir." Smythe didn't smile knowingly into the mirror. He simply inserted the earbud once more.

Monica turned, coming to life. "But I've still got work to do."

"The work you need to perform is to get yourself ready for your punishment tonight."

A tremble shimmied through her body. "How should I prepare?"

He leaned close, palming one breast. "A scented bubble bath. Shave your legs. Trim that sweet little pussy. Make yourself come. At least five times. Be ready for Smythe at eight."

She sucked her bottom lip. "What should I wear?"

A pity the corsets he'd purchased wouldn't be ready for a couple of weeks, but you shouldn't rush true artistry. "Your black high heels with the silver rivets along the side and the new stockings and lingerie." He thought of her clothing, the outfits which drew his eye more often. The ones that made his cock hard as he watched her leave his office. "The black pencil skirt and that sheer cream-colored blouse. But don't wear the camisole, just the white bra with the black lace we bought today."

She tilted her head, her eyes darkening. "That's very specific."

"You think I haven't watched you, Miss Dawson? You think I don't know every stitch of clothing you wear, the shoes that match, the skirts that cup your ass? I see everything."

She drew in a deep breath, her breasts rising. He was reminded of their succulent plumpness above the line of the corset. His mouth watered. He wanted a taste of her nipple to add to the ambrosia of her sweet pussy.

"What are you going to do to me?"

He smiled. And not in a nice way. "Punish you. In ways you could never imagine. For as long as I want. Until you beg."

He didn't say what she would beg for. He'd let her think on that. While she was in the tub. As she touched herself. When she came.

CHAPTER SEVEN

Monica planted her feet at the end of the claw foot tub, her hips rocking as she swirled her fingers in all her moisture. Biting her lip as the climax rolled through her, she collapsed, sending the water sloshing over the side onto the tile floor.

Five. Or maybe that was six. Monica had lost count of her orgasms.

Sean pounded on the door. "What the hell are you doing, Monica, overflowing the tub?"

She growled. "Butt out." When the hell had he gotten home? He was usually out late on a Friday night, *very* late.

"Let me in," he demanded.

"I'm taking a bath."

"Come on," he cajoled. "I've seen it all before."

She hadn't locked herself in, but even Sean respected the message behind a closed door. "Just wait a minute."

She was done bathing, shaving, trimming and climaxing according to Mr. Sutton's specifications. So Monica climbed out, rubbed down, then fastened the white bra with its sexy black lace and stepped into the matching thong.

Sean hadn't seen *all*, and she wasn't about to show him. Unfortunately, she hadn't brought the evening's outfit into the bathroom with her. Despite his sexual preference, he eyed her up and down as she left her steamy sanctuary.

"Nice. Very nice. The man has excellent taste in lingerie." Sniffing the air, he added, "You smell good, too." He tipped his head. "Maybe I need to find a cross-dresser so I can trick him out in pretty lingerie and douse him with sweetly scented bath stuff."

She slapped him lightly on the arm as she crossed to the bed where she'd laid her clothes. Her room was more solid than girlie, with a comforter and teal duvet on the queen-size bed, a dark wood bureau, and a chest of drawers. The side table lamp didn't have a frilly shade, and the windows weren't covered with lace curtains or matching valance, only ordinary blinds. She considered herself too no-nonsense for all that.

The only real luxury was the overstuffed chair Sean had thrown himself into. She'd chosen it to make a comfortable reading spot.

"I take it you're seeing the great man tonight."

She smoothed the thigh-highs over her freshly shaved legs. "He's sending a car at eight."

Sean whistled. "Stockings," he added in a low, seductive pitch, elongating the word. "Very sexy. You do realize he's going to fuck the hell out of you tonight."

"I have no idea." She was all keyed up from the orgasms, her skin jumping, and she wanted Mr. Sutton to take her more than anything. She wanted *him* to make her come. Technically, he'd made her come this afternoon against the wall, his tongue on her. But she'd hovered on the edge all day, and the orgasm had been more from the tension than his mouth. He'd licked her once, for God's sake, and she'd gone off like a volcano.

"It makes me hard thinking about it, you know."

"Would you stop," she said mildly, not truly bothered. Sean was all about sex, talking, thinking, musing, and she participated more than her fair share.

"I'd love to be a fly on the wall. To watch every dirty

thing he does to you." He shook a finger at her. "Sweetie, you have to swear to tell me."

She buttoned the sheer blouse and stepped into her skirt. "Maybe. If you've got a good story for me." She eyed him. "What'd you do to Jim today?"

He smiled slyly. "I cornered him in the copy room and wouldn't let him go until he said he'd meet me at the club tonight." He rolled his eyes. "He was so terrified someone would see that he agreed just to get out of there."

"Do you think he'll show?" She passed him on the way back to the bathroom to do her makeup. Talking with Sean had settled her nerves about her evening with Mr. Sutton.

He followed her to the doorway, rubbing his hands in glee. "No idea. But I love the anticipation." He winked at her in the mirror as she leaned forward to apply her eye shadow. "Interesting that I didn't have to tell him where the club is."

"You think he's been there before?"

"Maybe. But he's terrified of coming out of the closet. I don't get that. It's not like it's the dark ages and he'd be stoned to death if anyone figured out he was gay."

There was still intolerance. Sean had suffered it. She'd seen him shunned in high school for being who he was. Granted that was twenty years ago, but she didn't think society had come as far as it needed to. She figured you could gauge attitudes by the commercials you saw on TV, and so far, the All-American couple depicted in TV advertising was not the same gender. "You should have some sympathy for the guy."

Sean ignored her. "Of course, he could be bi," he mused. "He brought a girl to the Christmas party. But she could have been window dressing."

"You and I went to the prom together."

He snorted. "Right. Only because neither of us could find dates."

Not getting asked to the senior prom had been one of her more humiliating experiences. After all, missing the prom was social death. In the end, she'd had the absolute best time with Sean. He'd danced with all the girls and been the hit of the party. At least with the female half. That was Sean. He was good in his own skin. She hoped he'd find the right guy someday.

She scowled at his reflection in the mirror. "I don't know why you're bothering with Jim."

"Because it's fun. I love the intrigue. He's so uptight, which is why I love copping a feel in the copy room or doing the nasty in the men's room." He shrugged. "It'll get old eventually, but right now I'm dying for someone from work to see us together. It'll totally freak him out."

"You're cruel." But she couldn't help smiling at him. Sean's glee was infectious.

She glanced at her watch. "Oh my God, it's almost eight. I have to run."

She pushed Sean aside as she dashed through the bathroom door. She needed a purse. No, she didn't. But where would she carry her key? "Toss me the black pumps." She pointed to the closet. "The ones with the silver rivets."

Sean threw them to her. "It's like dressing Cinderella. You're totally hot in those shoes." Unlike a straight guy, he'd never cared that she was taller than him when she wore her heels.

She grabbed a clutch purse from a drawer, dropped in lipstick and her house key. At the last second, she added twenty bucks. A girl should never go anywhere without money in case she needed to make a quick getaway.

"Now stay up here. I don't want the driver to see you." She certainly didn't want Smythe telling Mr. Sutton there was a man in her flat.

"You're going to owe me for this," Sean called as she fled down the stairs. "Details. The real dirty ones."

She already had dirty details. Like what Mr. Sutton had done to her in the hall outside the sex shop. But after tonight…

She was already wet with the mere thought of tonight's

punishment.

⬤

Mr. Sutton's flat comprised the entire top floor of a Pacific Heights apartment building constructed after the 1906 earthquake. At night, the view was a blaze of lights from the Marina District and across the bay into Sausalito. The extravagant fireworks display for the Golden Gate's seventy-fifth anniversary would have been spectacular from his vantage point.

Monica wasn't given time to enjoy.

"You follow instructions well, Miss Dawson." He perused her outfit, which was exactly as ordered. He wore a business suit, black with a white shirt and red tie, and, as usual, he was scrumptious in the tailored fit. Since the work scenario was his chosen role play, he must have thought about it over the years she'd worked for him. That made their attire far sexier than see-through lace or tight leather.

"Come this way." He crooked a finger, leading her down a hallway of polished wood floors and intricate crown moldings. They left behind the living and dining room, with their expensive carpets and carved oriental furniture. The kitchen opened off to the right, all black, white, and chrome, pots and pans hanging from racks over a center island. She'd been to his home before, often organizing his social gatherings. She knew there were three bedrooms, one of which he used as a home office. There was also one locked room she'd never entered.

It was to this room he led her. The door was unlocked, as if he'd been preparing for her. "After you, Miss Dawson." He waved her in with a flourish.

She caught her breath as she surveyed his hidden room.

"Does it meet your expectations?"

She couldn't say what she'd been expecting. Torture devices, a whipping post? Not really. But this was almost ordinary. Until you looked more closely. Oak bookshelves and glass cabinets lined the walls. It was only once you stared at them that you realized they were filled with a variety of instruments, from assorted gags and floggers to dildos, handcuffs, leather hoods, and blindfolds. A flat-panel TV hung where one would expect a window. Stacks of DVDs and a player sat on a glass table. Then things got dicey. A chair with a hole in the seat was fitted with fur-lined leather ankle and wrist restraints. A suspension bar hung from the ceiling, with bolts in the hardwood floor below it. A cross, standing like a great X in the middle of the room, sported handcuffs at the end of each arm, including the feet. Restraints and grab bars outfitted a massage table with a face cradle. One end of the table had been let down, and the flogger he'd purchased lay ominously on the padded surface.

Not wanting to give him any clue to her thoughts, she backed away, threw an arm wide to encompass the shelves and cabinets. "Why did we need to buy anything? You have it all here." Every device imaginable, from anal beads and Ben Wa balls to butt plugs and nipple clamps. And more than one style of each.

"I'm a collector. I like the unique."

Was he collecting her, too? "But you don't use them?"

"I do." He was close again, his male scent twining around her like rope, binding her to him until all she could breathe in was him. "But you're special, and you deserve your very own."

That warmed her in more ways that sexual. Or had he said that to every woman he'd brought here? Did each instrument belong to a different submissive?

He opened a cabinet door and removed the spider gag. Her chest tightened.

"Hold this." He dangled it before her on one finger.

"No. Please."

His blue eyes turned glacial. "This is your threat. If you displease me, you get the spider gag. If you please me, you have nothing to worry about."

She reached up slowly. With the tip of his finger to hers, he let the device slide down onto her hand.

"It's all within your control," he whispered. "All you have to do is please me."

That was all she'd ever wanted to do. Now more than ever, after having had a taste of what he could give her, pleasing Mr. Sutton was all she cared about.

❧

She was like a doe in the headlights with no clue what to make of him. The spider gag, truth be told, had never been his thing. He wanted to feel a woman's lips wrap around him. *Her* lips. That particular device was like a glory hole. But he delighted in her wide eyes, her quickened breath, the anticipatory fear that made her pulse race. She needed a reason to do whatever he asked, and the gag represented that.

She was gorgeous in the sheer blouse, the black lace of the bra peeking through. Her hair fell over her shoulders in a sexy mass. Had he dreamed, over the years, of pulling the pins from her tidy bun and pushing his fingers through the thick golden locks? Yes, he had. But she'd always been off limits.

Monica was no longer off limits, and there were so many things he wanted to do to her.

"I'm going to unbutton your blouse." He wanted to feel his fingers brush her skin.

"Yes, Mr. Sutton," she said obediently, her hand still aloft, the gag dangling.

He felt her flesh warm with each button and each touch. Her breasts damn near overflowed the cups of the lace bra. The choice of lingerie had been an inspiration. He held back a groan of need as he pulled the blouse from her skirt, its lapels hanging open to frame her bounty.

"These are mine to touch," he said.

"Yes, Mr. Sutton."

He rimmed a finger along the brassiere. A nipple peaked just on the edge of the demi cup. He flicked lightly, once, twice, and watched her pupils dilate, her nostrils flaring slightly.

"Pinch your nipples for me." That was another of his delights, making her do things to herself for his pleasure. He could watch her expression when she was the one doing the touching.

Her gaze holding his, she dipped both hands into her lingerie and squeezed.

"Harder," he ordered.

Her lids drooped, her lips parted, a sigh whispered between them.

"Good," he told her. "You like it. Are you wet?" He could already smell her arousal and feel the heat flushing her skin.

"Yes." She forgot the proper address, but he didn't correct her.

"Turn around."

She presented her behind to him. He unzipped the skirt, pushed it down, his hands lingering on her hips and thighs as the material dropped to the floor. She stole his breath yet again. The woman was perfection, the round globes of her ass, the lush curves, her creamy skin.

He finished removing her clothes, tossing them onto the top of a glass cabinet. She stood before him in high heels and the pretty things he'd bought. He liked the stamp of ownership that buying her clothing gave him. Perhaps he should outfit her entire wardrobe.

She hadn't moved, hadn't asked another question. Nor did she try to cover herself. She was becoming comfortable with her nakedness in front of him.

"Give me the gag."

She grimaced slightly, but handed it over. Rounding the table he'd set in the center of the room, he laid the gag on the floor right below the face cradle. She would be able to see it like a warning. Not that she'd need it. She was going to love what he did to her.

He stood back to peruse her, stroking his chin. She shifted slightly from one foot to the other. "Panties or no panties?" he queried, more to himself than to her. "You're so fucking hot in that thong." Black lace over white satin, he could see the damp spot of her arousal. "Off," he finally said. "And the bra." He flicked his finger, indicating she should do it herself.

The sight of her naked but for the heels and skin-tone thigh-highs shot an electric jolt to his cock. "You are a prize, Miss Dawson," he murmured.

Then he picked up the flogger he'd purchased just for her. His heart beat hard against the wall of his chest, his hands perspired with anticipation, and his cock was an iron rod in his pants. "Now for your punishment. Bend over the table."

CHAPTER EIGHT

Monica hesitated only a moment, her legs trembling. But she remembered the gag and did what he told her to.

"Hold the rubber grips and put your face in the cradle." He buckled the fur-lined restraints around her wrists while below her lay the threat of the spider gag.

He moved behind her. "Spread your legs." Tapping her shoe with his own, he ordered, "Wider." Then he restrained her ankles.

She was spread-eagled, exposed, and oh so wet for him. She could barely breathe as need rushed through her. The orgasms in the tub had only whet her appetite. The sex talk with Sean had heightened it. Mr. Sutton's light touch on her breasts had made her burn, especially after he'd told her she was special enough to rate her own toys. But the zing through her entire body as she pinched her nipples for him brought her to the brink in a single second.

Now she needed to solve the mysteries of the things he did with his women. The pain, the pleasure, the—

She screamed as his hand connected hard with her bottom, the sting racing through her flesh, up her spine. "Oh my God," she gasped. Then he smacked her again.

She cried out once more. But something else was

happening, not just the pain, but a pulse of pleasure. His fingers were on her, almost in her, slapping her sensitized flesh. She panted. Again and again he found a spot between her spread legs that made her body shudder.

"When it hurts too much," he told her, "squeeze the handles, and the pain will recede."

She alternately squeezed and released the handles, but only to keep herself steady on the table. Somehow the small movements accentuated the sensations. Her butt stung, but her pussy throbbed. She groaned but it wasn't pain. It was beyond pain, indescribable.

"You filthy girl, I do believe you love it."

She wanted more. He gave her another smack that reverberated through her body and released a gush of moisture.

"Christ," he said with near reverence.

His words were followed by a new sensation, the whack of the flogger. Monica screamed. It hurt, oh God, it did. Yet her pussy contracted and wept for more. He smacked her buttocks, the tops of her thighs, and that glorious thwack right between her spread legs. It was tingling, burning, stinging, hot, and excruciatingly sweet.

She couldn't remember Ms. Hopkins' words, only the look on her face as she described the sensations, and Monica understood completely. She probably wouldn't sit down for a week without feeling it. And she would remember that the pleasure was so much greater than the pain.

Her body shuddered with the rhythm of his punishment. Each time she shot closer to the pinnacle. Her legs were like jelly and tears leaked from her eyes.

He worked her and backed off, brought her to the very precipice, then pulled her back. Hard and fast, then slow and lingering, almost sweet. Rising, falling, on the edge, then two steps back. He kept her riding the line between pleasure and pain, between want and need, but never letting her go the whole way.

He made her crazed with need. "Please, please, please," she begged.

Then he was standing in front of her, everything stopped, everything gone, not even the edge of ecstasy anymore. "Please," she whispered.

"Look at me."

She raised herself with a grip on the rubber handles.

He laid the flogger on her back and undid his suit jacket. "Please what?"

"Please don't stop. Please let me come. Fuck me. Take me. Whatever you want."

A sheen of sweat covered his face as he removed his jacket and threw it across the punishment chair with the hole in it. "You want me to fuck you?"

"Yes, God, yes, please." The tears hovered in her voice.

He yanked off his tie, tossed it, and rolled his sleeves to his elbows. "I don't think you're ready for that."

"I am. I swear it." She'd even let him use the spider gag as long as he fed her his cock. Her butt was stinging loudly, the pleasure gone, desire just beyond her reach. "Please."

"You're not done being punished."

She couldn't remember what she'd done to deserve punishment in the first place.

"You're not looking at me."

"I am." She couldn't take her eyes off him.

He palmed the front of his slacks. "Do you see how hard you make me?"

She saw what she'd done to him. He bulged in his pants, hard, thick, huge. She imagined she could see him pulse.

"That's what your punishment does to me. The more you get, the more I like it. Don't ever forget that. I like making you scream. I like seeing your bottom turn red with the imprint of my hand or the lash of the flogger." He stroked himself for her. "But you haven't earned my cock yet. You have a long way to go before you deserve that, my dear."

She wanted to cry. He'd driven her to the top, and now

he refused. Was this submission? Or was it torture?

He crossed to a bookshelf in front of her, his body obscuring the devices stored there, and made a selection. Then he turned. "You can have this instead."

She couldn't see what he held. A paddle? A nipple clamp? Oh God, please, not a butt plug.

Then he filled her with something long and silicon, and turned it on. It buzzed inside her, vibrating straight through to her clitoris. She let her upper body drop to the table.

"You'll have to be satisfied with the dildo, my dear. Until you prove yourself worthy of my cock."

Then he brought the flogger down on her. It didn't start small or soft, it was simply there, back and forth across her bottom, slapping the sweet spot between her legs while the vibrator hummed inside. She rode from one orgasmic wave to the next, her hands flexing on the handles. Tears dripped down onto the spider gag below. And still her body quaked for him. She screamed for him. She cried for him.

Until she was completely lost in him.

❧

One hand on the wall, Rance leaned into the shower, letting the water beat down on his head. He could still smell her despite the incessant sluice over his body.

She was amazing. She tested his strength, his limits. She'd worked her way into his head. If he didn't believe in his own sense of control, he might have said he was obsessed with her.

He turned, the stinging spray hitting his buttocks. Another reminder of her. She'd become a wild thing, begging for her punishment, for the climax. He'd observed first-timers before, and they never took to the hand, let alone a flogger, with the exuberance she'd shown. The red imprint on her gorgeous ass had enflamed him and taken him to new heights. He'd had women who wanted it harder, begged him to draw blood, in fact. He'd even gone so far as to imagine one of his wives in their place, which had added to the thrill. But none had been as pleasurable as his beautiful secretary. He hadn't beaten her hard. The marks of the flogger had faded by the time she'd left, and in the morning the evidence would be gone. But it wasn't about hard blows. It was about how long he could keep his woman straddling the line between pleasure and pain, how far he could take her as she begged for more, wanted more, needed it. He'd achieved that delicate balance with Monica until she'd simply detonated. In that moment, he'd wanted her so badly his hands had shaken with need.

He could still feel her silky skin beneath his fingers, smell the sweet, hot scent of her arousal. And see the red prints of his palm on her creamy flesh.

Rance stroked his cock, the sting of water like nails raking his back.

Thank God he'd secured her wrists to the table. If not, he'd have put her hand on him. And once that happened, he'd have been in her mouth. There would have been no resisting.

But she wasn't ready for him yet. She wasn't ready to do whatever he desired. She wouldn't drop to her knees and suck another cock for him simply because he wanted to watch. She wouldn't let a woman lick her to orgasm for his voyeuristic pleasure. She wouldn't take another man's hand on her ass wielding the punishment. A submissive needed to be loaned out. Monica wasn't a loaner yet.

He wasn't sure he could wait until she was before he had her. Even now, he could close his eyes and imagine the feel of her mouth on him. Christ, he wanted it. Badly. So fucking badly that his balls were tight and ready. For her.

But that wasn't how he worked a woman. He spanked her, flogged her, taught her the discipline required, loaned her to others. Then, finally, she would be ready for him. His submissives had always loved his training. It freed them to fuck any man they wanted. Because he told them it was what *he* wanted. It was about power, and the feeling was mutual.

His women wanted to give him the power. It got them off as much as it did him.

He saw Monica in his mind's eye, spread-eagled on a bed, impaled, fucked, screaming with the pleasure of it all. And her eyes on him as she came.

He threw his head back and groaned, pumping his fist faster.

"Take me," he whispered. "All of me." Her lips slid over his crown, her hand squeezed his balls, her fingers stroked his length. The explosion started deep and blew him sky high. He shouted out his pleasure in guttural cries, his climax arcing across the shower to be washed away by the pounding water.

He leaned heavily against the wall, catching his breath.

Yes, he wanted his new submissive badly. How long could he hold out?

Monica snuggled beneath the comforter, hidden under cover of darkness.

"He spanked you, flogged you, made you come, then simply helped you dress and sent you off with his driver after telling you to be ready for a damn business trip on Monday? Like you're *just* his secretary?" Sean was horrified.

It hadn't been as bad as that. Mr. Sutton had petted her, praised her, told her how beautiful she was, how perfectly she'd come for him, how magnificently she'd accepted her punishment. He'd caressed her as he helped her dress, buttoned her blouse, zipped her skirt. But he had sent her off after reminding her *and* Smythe that he was to pick her up at four-thirty on Monday morning for their Chicago flight. And Sean was ruining it all. "Stop it. The night was amazing."

Sean started to sing *Don't Rain On My Parade.* Monica slapped his arm. "Get out of my bed."

He ignored her order. "Okay, so tell me how a normal

woman with normal desires can like having a man flog her?"

"It didn't hurt."

"Right." His disgust filled the dark.

"I'm serious. It didn't hurt in a bad way." Her body ached, but more from the power of that orgasm than the spanking or the flogging. She still tingled. That was the only way to describe it. Her skin burned, and the sensation made her want to touch herself.

"All right, sweetie, then let me just say there's got to be something wrong with a man who gets off on giving a woman pain."

"It wasn't like that either." She remembered Mr. Sutton's impassioned speech, how the red heat of her spanked flesh made him hot. His words had nearly sent her over the edge. "I just can't describe it to you. It's not about getting off on pain. Because it actually feels good." She was, however, forced to add, "In a weird sort of way." It was incredibly intimate.

"I worry about your job when this is all over."

She'd do her best to make sure it was never over. But she couldn't say that to Sean. He'd say she was in over her head, that her expectations were whacked. That Mr. Sutton would leave her like he'd left all his women, including his two wives.

The difference was that Monica was indispensable in his office. And she would make herself indispensable in his private BDSM dungeon as well.

If she said *that*, Sean would ask her why. He'd ask if she was in love with her boss. Sean was her best friend, but even best friends kept secrets from each other, and she wasn't about to tell him how she felt about Mr. Sutton. Was this craving anything like love?

"I'm not worried about my job for now. I'm too valuable. It would take him forever to train someone else to do what I do." Especially now that she'd proven how good she was on his flogging table. "Why don't we talk about you and Jim?"

Sean flopped over on his back, throwing an arm dramatically over his eyes. "Fuck, it was hot. He was a wild man."

"No way."

"Swear it. We met at the club, I got a few drinks in him, he started dancing. Not with me, but in general, because everyone's out on the floor, ya know."

"Jim? Your *conservative* living-in-the-closet Jim?"

"Yeah, that one. I moseyed up behind him and starting doing a really sweet bump and grind. Christ, I was hard, Monica, you wouldn't believe it." He took a dramatic pause.

Monica made the obligatory gasp. "And?"

"I grabbed him by the wrist and dragged him off into an alcove. Then I tore at his jeans and went down on my knees right there and took his cock in my mouth."

Excitement rippled through her. "Oh my God. No one could see you?"

He snickered. "There's a lot of little hideaways at the club."

"And he let you do it?"

"He went crazy. He practically fucked my mouth, holding my head, groaning, moaning. It was so fucking hot. I swallowed his whole goddamn load, so fucking sweet you wouldn't believe." He sighed, stretched, and almost purred as if he'd just had an orgasm. "I want more."

Monica understood the sentiment. She wanted so much more. She was sure after tonight Mr. Sutton would give it to her. She'd pleased him. But he still hadn't come. He hadn't forced her to suck him. He hadn't taken her. Despite the fact that she was right there for the taking.

"It was fucking amazing," Sean went on. "But of course, on Monday he'll pretend like it never happened. Like he doesn't even know my name let alone had his cock in my mouth." He dropped his voice. "Until I corner him in the file vault and put my hand down his pants. Then he'll be screaming my name."

"He's had it once. Now he knows what it's like, he'll

want more," Monica agreed.

Just like Mr. Sutton would need more. But why didn't he touched her beyond the spanking? He couldn't be impotent. He'd been so hard tonight as he stood in front of her.

"I've got plans for Jim. I love the whole sneaking around thing. It really gets me off."

Everyone had a special thing that got him off. What was Mr. Sutton's? What could she do that would incite him to the extent that he simply couldn't help himself, that he *had* to have her?

"It's going to be harder getting Jim to suck me. I've got to make him want it more than he's afraid of it."

Yes, she had to make Mr. Sutton want it. Unless he didn't actually want her? Maybe there was something wrong with her. No, she'd heard desire in his voice. Holding out was just part of the submission and dominance game. Not allowing himself an orgasm meant he was in control.

"What are you going to do, Sean?" she asked even as she was thinking about Mr. Sutton.

"I'll keep pushing him. Showing him how good it feels. Until he figures out how much better it will feel if he goes all the way."

Right. That's what she had to do. Keep pushing Mr. Sutton until he lost control.

CHAPTER NINE

The business trip. It was perfect. Monica always booked a room adjoining Mr. Sutton's. So that she could be at his beck and call. They'd boarded a six a.m. flight to Chicago on Monday morning. Monica had been making her plans all weekend.

She'd worn a stylish gray herringbone suit with a short, tailored jacket over a form-fitting pencil skirt that hit her midcalf. The slit, however, went all the way up to midthigh. She paired it with black thigh-highs, the lace at the top just visible through the slit when she took a seat.

Mr. Sutton did not so much as notice a strand of hair out of place, let alone her overexposed thigh—and she was sure to display it—as they settled into their first-class seats. He took the window seat, as usual, and she got the aisle. That way she didn't disturb him when she used the restroom. Except this morning. She wanted to disturb him, wanted him to notice her. She just plain *wanted*. But he was all business, pulling papers from his briefcase, going over the agenda for the board meeting he was to attend, making notes. When she ordered a mimosa to go with her breakfast, he simply looked at her over his reading glasses as he dictated correspondence into a recorder. Later she would use a voice recognition software to transfer them all to her computer and prepare them for distribution.

They worked together like they always worked together. As if he hadn't spanked her or flogged her. As if he hadn't tasted her in the sex shop's hallway at the bottom of the stairs. As if he hadn't made her come. For God's sake, he hadn't even asked if she'd given herself her quota of orgasms on Saturday and Sunday. Monica had added one this morning while she was in the shower, just for good measure.

She shifted in her seat. Her bottom still tingled, a pleasant burn that reminded her of Friday night. It had made her aware of him all weekend, the phantom feel of his hand, his scent, his voice.

Didn't he know he was driving her absolutely insane as he sat next to her pretending nothing had happened, their conversation completely business-oriented?

She sighed heavily. He ignored her.

Finally the interminable flight was over. They collected their carry-ons. Monica had arranged for a car, which was waiting for them when they exited the terminal. August in Chicago was sweltering, and she was glad for the air-conditioned comfort. Mr. Sutton checked his emails during the half-hour drive to the facility, a manufacturing company on the outskirts of Chicago for whom Mr. Sutton had sat on the board for the past year. His background was in high-tech manufacturing.

It had always been like this when she traveled with him. She'd just wanted...more. She'd wanted to join the mile-high club with him in the first-class bathroom. Or at least to put a blanket over his lap while she unzipped his slacks.

But there'd been nothing. He was maddening. Last week had been nonstop action. Now this, absolutely nothing.

They checked in with the receptionist, received their visitor badges, and stowed their luggage in a small closet behind the desk before heading up the stairs to the board room.

Evan Kenton, CEO, stood by the double doors like a greeter. A handsome man in his midfifties with steel gray hair, he was fit, tall, and sharp-witted.

He held out a hand. "Sutton. Miss Dawson. I trust you had a good flight."

Only Mr. Sutton shook. The hand wasn't offered to Monica. She was merely an appendage.

There were five other board members including the chairman, Mr. Litfield. Only one was female. They were interchangeable with the other boards of which Mr. Sutton was a member. The executives would troop through for their departmental presentations. It wasn't a quarter-end, no financials to review, and the meeting would be routine.

Coffee was served, the board members milled about for a few minutes exchanging polite chitchat, while Monica was relegated to a comfortable chair along the wall rather than at the conference table. Her job was to take notes and gather impressions. Was there something about which Evan Kenton seemed nervous? Did an executive appear to be hiding anything? It was amazing how many staff members believed the board was the enemy. She didn't count Evan Kenton among that type, but Mr. Sutton required her vigilance.

The board room was well appointed but not opulent, with utilitarian blue carpeting, not too thick but not so thin as to wear quickly. The table was oak and the chairs covered in fabric. The coffee bar sported a sink, small fridge, and a Keurig coffee machine that brewed individual cups. Kenton's secretary had handled the distribution, circling the room with mugs and creamers. She'd also served Monica with no bias.

Both the facility and the room had met with Mr. Sutton's approval. He didn't like company money wasted on luxuries, and while he was reimbursed for his travel, he submitted his expenses at an economy rate rather than the first class in which he preferred to travel.

"Miss Dawson," her boss said, his hand raised

imperiously. "I have a brief task requiring your attention." She rose. He met her halfway. She noted Kenton's eyes on them. She'd noted his eyes on her thigh when she'd been seated. Which was more than she'd received from Mr. Sutton.

Without touching her, Mr. Sutton leaned close. It wasn't an intimate gesture, simply secretive, as if he didn't want his cohorts in the room privy to his business.

His breath fluttering strands of hair at her temples, he whispered close to her ear. "Pick up your phone and leave the room. Go to the ladies' room and remove your panties. Then return, take your seat, and cross your legs."

⟨❧⟩

Monica stared a moment too long before saying, "Yes, Mr. Sutton." Then did exactly as he told her.

He allowed himself a slight smile. She'd fidgeted the entire flight, shifting in her seat, retrieving lotion from her purse, a nail file, moving a paper one way, then another. All the while, that sliver of thigh-high stocking peeped out at him, beckoning. His fingers itched to push aside the skirt, to touch, to wander.

That's exactly what the little wench wanted. He'd denied her. Until the moment he told her to take off her panties. That order, of course, revealed everything, how aware he was of every move she made, how badly he wanted to steep all his senses in her.

His suit jacket disguised his erection as he turned back to Kenton. "A small matter I forgot," he offered as explanation. Of course, he had the reputation of never forgetting a thing. "You were saying?" He also knew what Kenton had been discussing, his recent cruise to the Galapagos Islands. Rance agreed that it sounded quite amazing. Then his mind had naturally drifted to Monica stretched out on deck in a thong bikini, skin shimmering with suntan oil, hair spread out around her.

"Don't you agree?" Kenton asked.

"Definitely," Rance agreed to whatever, while in his mind he ticked off the minutes until Monica returned.

"Taken care of, Mr. Sutton," she murmured as she passed him. He scented arousal, her particular hot and spicy ambrosia. His mouth watered as he remembered the taste he'd had of her. Not enough.

"Thank you," he said graciously. As a dom, he wouldn't thank his submissive, but this was a professional setting.

Kenton's eyes were glued to the hint of lace thigh-high visible through the slit in Monica's skirt as she resumed her seat. She'd worn the outfit to work before, but Rance couldn't remember the slit riding quite so high. Or perhaps it was the stockings that made all the difference.

There was a split second lull in Kenton's conversation. His nostrils flared slightly as if he, too, detected her aroma. Then he tore his gaze away, glanced at his watch, and raised his voice to say, "I believe it's time we got started."

The chairman, Litfield, sat at the table's head, Kenton on his left. Like Rance, Litfield was a member of numerous boards. In his seventies, he was as sharp as a man half his age.

Rance took the chair next to the CEO. He'd placed Monica strategically, directly across from them. Beside him, Kenton pushed his chair back and slightly to the right. Rance followed the line of sight. Straight to Monica's legs. Her skirt fell on either side of her knee, revealing the black lace through that delicious slit.

He willed her to pull a Sharon Stone and recross her legs, but she was retrieving her notepad and pen from her briefcase. She would write down notes, comments, and observations for his review later. She had at first wanted to use her electronic organizer to skip the transcription, but he'd always believed people were less forthcoming if they thought you were recording every word they said. She'd therefore purchased software that would allow her to scan in the notes. So efficient. So intelligent. So damn sexy.

Litfield opened with a general discussion of the quarter and the upcoming product release in October, just in time for the holiday purchasing season. Kenton was attentive, answered appropriately, putting off questions which would be covered in the product management presentation to come later in the day. Yet Rance was aware of the occasional straying glance in Monica's direction. She pretended to be oblivious.

Rance, however, knew the signs, she was anything but. Recrossing her legs, the sly little wench managed to hold her notepad strategically positioned to hide the view.

She'd have to be punished for that.

Of course, if she'd really flashed the board, there might be hell to pay. He'd ordered her to remove the panties because it was exceptionally hot to know she was naked under the skirt. And because it reminded her to whom she belonged. She was owned. She was his.

They took a break as Kenton signaled his secretary to notify the first VP that they were ready for his presentation. There were coffee refills. When Monica rose, Kenton was on her, giving her first dibs at the coffee machine, plus a little small talk.

Kenton was married. He'd never chitchatted with Monica. But then she'd never worn that skirt and stockings to a board meeting before. She smiled, her eyes shifting to Rance, flitting back to Kenton. Then she actually took a step closer, moving into his personal space. The move lasted fifteen seconds—Rance counted—then she shifted away, giving Kenton access to the coffee pods. He actually felt a flutter of jealousy low in his gut. And it began to grow as he watched her.

Dirty girl. She was flirting. Right in front of her boss and master.

This definitely required punishment. Especially since he'd brought the tools of his trade with him. She wouldn't sit down for a week.

She was not invited to the dinner that night. It was board members and executives only. Monica had gotten used to being excluded from certain social functions even though she'd always felt it was a tad rude. Mr. Sutton, on the other hand, had never insisted on her attendance, primarily because it was a company expense, and he didn't believe in overcharging. Secretaries simply weren't included. Sean said it was because they were second-class citizens.

Monica simply felt it was business. If ever asked, she begged off, and tonight she was glad for the respite from work. She ordered room service, then ran a scented bubble bath, preparing herself for her master. He'd stated an intention when he told her to remove her panties. She'd been wet and ready in that hours-long meeting. Her concentration had sucked. She'd definitely have to spruce up the notes she'd scanned in when she arrived back at the hotel. But she had a suspicion the state of her commentary wouldn't be an issue tonight. What Mr. Sutton would do to her was a mystery, but the fact that he'd do something was inevitable. She was so ready, her skin smooth and scented, five orgasms under her belt. But she needed more. Hmm, how many could she fit in before he returned? Her fingers worked, the water rippling with her moves.

"What the hell are you doing?"

Her eyes flew open as she sat up abruptly, water streaming down her breasts and sloshing over the tub edge. She'd left her connecting door open, and Mr. Sutton now filled the bathroom entry, tall, breathtakingly handsome, impossibly stern. He lasered her with his blue eyes, and his gaze burned right through her.

"I was giving myself the orgasms you ordered. You said every night." She let a meekness settle into her voice, perfect for what she considered a submissive should be. But she didn't sink back down beneath the bubbles. He'd removed his suit jacket, and all the evidence indicated that he enjoyed the sight. How long had he been watching her before he spoke?

"I didn't tell you to do it when you're with me." His voice was a delicious growl that hummed inside her.

"I wasn't with you," she protested. "You were having dinner. I was here alone."

He narrowed his eyes. "Are you complaining?"

"Of course not." Sort of. Sean was talking through her mouth.

"I'll give you five minutes to dry off, then be in my room. Do not put on one stitch of clothing." He turned on the heel of his polished shoes.

Monica scrambled up to grab a towel and climbed out. Her excitement bubbled like the shimmering froth on the surface of her bath water. Was he really angry? Had she done something wrong? Or was this part of his game? He had to manufacture something for which she deserved punishment.

She turned her watch on the marble counter and counted out her five minutes as she dried and lotioned in fast mode. She didn't dare be a second late.

He was showering. Monica felt her knees go weak. His body through the clear glass was toned and muscled. Then he turned to wash the shampoo from his hair, his head back, the long column of his throat leading down to his lightly furred chest with an arrow of hair pointing her in the right direction. She had to put a hand on the door jamb to steady herself. Mr. Sutton was utterly magnificent, his cock jutting, thick, long, and so hard it would be like riding steel to the top of her womb. Maybe even her heart.

She couldn't say how long she stood stock still, mesmerized by him. She'd always found him attractive. But the Greek god physique in the shower was beyond her wildest expectations.

The water slammed off, and he stared her down. "Get me a towel."

A polite *please* would have ruined the effect.

Monica yanked a towel from the rack and opened the shower door. Steam swirled in the air, carrying the scent of soap and shampoo. Mr. Sutton stepped onto the mat, rivulets of water running down his impressive body. He held her gaze for five seconds without taking the towel. "Dry me off."

She found it hard to breathe, hard to swallow. He was too perfect for words. Reaching up, she started with his hair simply because that's how she always did it. Covering his head with the towel, she massaged water from his hair. Moving down, she mopped his shoulders, chest, and abdomen, reveling in the hard muscles beneath the fluffy towel. Reaching around, she held the towel in both hands to swipe it across his back. The motion pulled him close, his cock rubbing her belly, overwhelmingly hard yet the skin delicately soft. She pressed close to dry off his butt, her head tipped back to lock eyes. Not a muscle of his face twitched. But his cock flexed between them.

Monica did what she'd dreamed of for five years. She dropped to her knees on the mat in front of him. He bobbed free before her lips, inviting. She wrapped the terry cloth around his cock and stroked him dry, resisting the irresistible lure of sliding her lips around him.

She sawed the towel between his legs, drying his sack and beyond. He inhaled, his abdomen expanding with a deep belly breath. His thighs, his knees, his calves, then finally she dabbed at his feet. And lifted her face to him.

She let her gaze beg.

He was unrelenting. "On the end of my bed," he directed. "Hands and knees. Head up, ass in the air."

It sounded like some sort of show-dog stance. Monica rushed to assume the position.

He entered, the thick hotel robe belted at his waist, its sleeves rolled up. Stopping at the end of the bed, he surveyed her. "Did you want him?"

She pulled her head up. "Who?"

He smacked her butt, her skin rippling, a shock of

pleasure-pain zinging to her clitoris.

"Did you want to suck his cock?"

What on earth was he talking about? "Who?"

The next swat swept through her entire body as his fingers connected solidly with her pussy, slipping inside a brief, intense moment. She almost fell to her elbows. Her eyes closed. She bit her lip. The moan clogged her throat.

"Did you think about fucking him?" he murmured, soft, low, deadly.

"Who?" she whispered, consumed with anticipation, fear, and need.

He slapped her again, but this time he wrapped his palm around her, covering her pussy, his index finger sliding through her parted folds and landing right on her clitoris.

Her whole body quaked, and she rocked back. A groan rose up. "Who?" she begged.

"Were you picturing him while you frigged yourself in the tub?" He smacked her.

"Who? Who? Who?" she hooted, urging him on, taking every swat, relishing it, begging for more even as he gave it to her, peppering her with questions, instructions. Curses.

"I pick your other men, not you. I tell you who to fuck. Dirty bitch. Can't get enough, can you. Always needing more."

She fell to her elbows, giving him total access. His touch turned her mindless. She didn't care who he was talking about or what her imagined sin could be. It didn't matter. There was only this, his hand on her, over and over, his fingers stroking her, making her crazy.

Until he stopped. Just like that. Stopped. When she'd been on the edge of orgasm. As if he'd scented it in the air, felt it in her juice, recognized it in the quiver of her limbs.

"Please," she begged.

"On your knees," he roared.

Just the sound almost made her come. Almost there, right on the ledge.

She scrambled off the bed, stumbling when her knees

gave out, and fell before him.

"Undo my robe," he snarled with displeasure. Then he licked his fingers, erasing the evidence of what he'd done to her. Yet there was something in his eyes, a hot flame. It wasn't just about punishment. It wasn't just about getting her scent on him. He wanted her taste. Maybe even needed it.

She unbelted him, and his cock sprang free. The crown was a raw, needy purple, and his testicles were full and tight. He wanted this. As badly as she did. The rest was just window dressing, an attempt to put her in her place. But his cock told it all.

She didn't take him in her mouth. He hadn't ordered her yet.

"I own you. You're mine. I dictate everything. Prove you're *my* slave." He raised an imperious brow. "If you're good enough, I just might let you suck Kenton. So you'll realize how worthless he is."

Evan Kenton? Was he crazy? She hadn't been flirting. She'd been polite. She'd worn the skirt to entice Mr. Sutton. Evan Kenton was just a by-product. Okay, yes, it was nice to finally be noticed after you'd been little more than a wall fixture. But she hadn't been flirting by any stretch of the imagination.

No, she hadn't done anything wrong at all. Yet Mr. Sutton was jealous. Oh my God, yes, he was. He really was.

She licked her lips, met his gorgeous cock eye-to-eye, and said, "This is what I want. CEO Kenton can go screw himself."

Then she took him in her mouth. His taste almost made her weep. Salty yet sweet. His skin was soft just as she'd thought, and smooth. A vein throbbed against her tongue, and his crown was like velvet stretched tight and thin.

She took him all the way, and he filled her completely. Cupping his tight balls in her palm, she squeezed gently as she slid her tongue back up the length of him. She doubled-teamed him with both hands, palpating his testicles and wrapping a fist around his shaft, stroking to match the rhythm of her lips encircling him.

She needed to swallow all of him, every last inch. He was too big to fit, but his length allowed her to touch him as well, to wallow in him, from the musky scent of his male skin to the silky pubic hair against her nose and the feel of him on her skin. The crinkly hair of his legs caressed her nipples.

She knew she had him when drops of pre-come bathed her tongue and his legs started to tremble.

CHAPTER TEN

"Christ."

His head was about to explode. Both of them. Monica Dawson had a mouth on her that would bring a better man than him to his knees.

She'd driven him to distraction this afternoon. His uncharacteristic jealousy had grown to the point that he could think of nothing but dragging her up on that conference table and staking his claim in front of everyone, especially Kenton, after Rance had bloodied his face.

He was breathing hard, his skin flushed hot. "Stop."

She didn't.

Pushing her back on her haunches, he spread his legs to steady himself. His limbs felt weak. "I think you're enjoying this a little too much."

So was he. That was the problem. He'd been about to lose his mind and his control. He'd intended to use the flogger on her. And a paddle. Yet when the moment of her punishment came, all he'd wanted was to get his hands on her in any way he could. He smelled her all over him. Her taste lingered on his tongue after he'd licked his fingers clean of her. Maybe that had been his undoing. Or maybe it was the way she trembled for him when his hand connected with her bottom. Or the gush of her pleasure on his fingers. Hell, it was everything. Which was why he had to stop her mouth from taking him completely.

He backed away from her, then realized that could interpreted as retreat. So he turned to rummage through his open carryon. Tossing aside her special flogger and the paddle, he held up what he wanted—what he *needed*—and turned back to her.

He'd left on only the bedside lamp and her hazel eyes darkened in the dim lighting. "Please. No. Not the spider gag. You promised."

"I did no such thing." He narrowed his eyes. "Don't question me. However, I will tell you this is not the spider gag. It's an O-ring. Which you didn't object to." He would have brought the spider, but where the O-ring was plastic, the spider was metal. With the hooks, security at the airport terminal probably would have deemed it a weapon. Handcuffs stayed behind for the same reason. He produced the zip ties with his other fist. "Hands behind you. Lace your wrists."

"Please."

"If you hadn't liked sucking me so much, you wouldn't need to be punished further." *He'd* like it too much. He'd been too close to going wild on her. He needed the O-ring gag and the ties to maintain distance.

Otherwise, it was akin to her mouth making love to his cock. That's how he'd thought of it. And that's why it had to stop. He didn't make love, and no woman made love to him. With her mouth or anything else. He also didn't become jealous of his submissives. Though this wasn't jealousy per se. It was the fact that he hadn't enjoyed her assets himself. He'd be damned if he'd let someone else have her before he did. She was his, after all. Later he'd loan her out. She'd love it. Most women he'd been with did. It was total permission to get nasty. They could even tell themselves they were forced. It was a no-guilt proposition.

"You're not moving," he said sternly.

She put her hands behind her back. He rounded to her lovely backside and restrained her. Then he stood in front of her.

His cock twitched as she pressed her lips firmly together. He loved submission, but he liked a little fight, too. "Open. Your. Mouth." Each word was a separate order.

Staring mutely, she tilted her chin in defiance.

He held her nose with his fingers. She gasped, opened her mouth to scream, and he slapped the ring in. Christ, she was good. Good at sucking—superlative, in fact—good at her job—superlative there, too—and just plain fucking good at making every single sex act better than he'd imagined.

He secured the gag behind her head and stepped back to survey his work. She sat on her haunches, her spine straight, her hands pulled behind. Her lips were parted in the large round O of the ring, which forced her to keep her mouth open and accessible.

"I've a mind to fuck your dirty little mouth," he said.

Her eyes narrowed, her nostrils flared. He stroked her under the chin. "I put my cock through this ring, and I fuck you. You're at my mercy. You take everything. You can't stop me." He leaned close, breathing her in, closing his eyes, and whispered, "You won't even want to stop me. And you'll swallow every drop."

"I hae ooh," she said, her speech slurred by the ring.

"I'm your master. You can't hate me. You agreed to everything. And you know you deserve this for disobeying me."

Her gaze blazed. Then he cupped his hand behind her head, pulled her up, and fed his cock to her mouth.

Holy hell. The warm recesses caressed him, stoked the fire that he'd temporarily banked. He gave it to her slowly, foregoing a deeper penetration until she got used to him. Holding her head in his hands, he restricted her movement and pumped his hips leisurely. Yes, he was in control. It was good, fucking good, but he could have stopped at any time.

He tipped his head back and increased his pace. She sucked in her cheeks on the out-pump and swirled her tongue around his length as he slid back in. The O-ring didn't prevent the caress. Somehow it seemed to enhance the slip-slide up and down his shaft. His legs began to quake. He told himself that was due to the slight bend in his knee to meet her height, forcing him to tense his thighs. His buttocks clenched with every thrust. His balls were hard and tight, aching. Christ, he wanted her hands on them, that sweet squeeze. Then he wasn't holding her head at all, as if his hands had simply fallen away. He thrust, she took. She sucked, drew out his essence. He gasped for air, his breath panting in his throat. How did she do that? How *could* she do it, turning him inside out?

His knees gave way, and she followed him down. As he leaned back on his hands, she fucked his cock, sucked him until he lost all control to her. There was only her mouth, that beautiful, succulent, sweet mouth, not her hands or her pussy or toys, nothing but her hot mouth. His hips bucked of their own volition, and his seed suddenly gushed from the depths of his soul. He shouted out, God only knew what, unintelligible words, curse words, maybe her name. And then he was simply lost in the climax, in her.

⊙≪≫

"Fuck, Monica, sweet God, Monica, hell, Monica." A gasp, a groan. "Monica."

She lost count of how many times he said her name. He filled her mouth, poured down her throat. She took it all. She took *him*.

Even as he collapsed to the carpet, she caressed him with her mouth, her tongue. She soothed the tremors, leaning her face to the side and nuzzling her nose into the crook of his thigh.

With the O-ring in place, she'd thought his cock would gag her. She'd thought it would be like having her mouth raped. But she'd known nothing. It was total freedom. She didn't have to give. She only had to take and accept.

It was all about perception.

Her bottom tingled from the spanking, and she hadn't had her orgasm. Her mouth was gagged and her hands bound, the zip ties cutting into her flesh, but she didn't care a whit. Because he'd given her everything when he let himself go. Ah victory, it was as sweet as the taste of his come.

His breathing was a steady rhythm now, and when she glanced along the length of his body, his eyes were closed. He hadn't fallen asleep, had he? Not now, at the moment of her triumph. It wasn't possible. It was actually humiliating.

The gag was starting to give her lockjaw. She might start drooling, too, because she couldn't swallow well with her mouth stuck open. She had a mind to kick him.

Then he drew a breath deep into his belly. "That was exceptional, Miss Dawson." He lifted his head, his eyes heavy lidded. "Where did you learn your skills?" There was humor in the cadence of his words.

She gave him a mumbled response. "Uk ooh." Which could have been either *Thank you* or *Fuck you*. She'd let him work that out for himself.

He sat up, the robe falling open around him, exposing everything. Despite the climax, he was still semihard. "Do you feel you've learned your lesson? Have you been punished enough?"

She nodded.

"Would you like the gag and the ties removed?"

This time she nodded vigorously. If she were truthful, she would have preferred the fur-lined cuffs. Or a scarf. The plastic ties were like something TV mobsters used on a victim when they forced him to kneel and shot him execution style.

Why did the aftermath of sex always go downhill? Even good sex. *Exceptional* sex.

He rose, entered the bathroom, returning a moment

later with a pair of nail scissors. Holding them up, he said, "Had to buy these earlier in the hotel shop." He snipped through the plastic.

Monica massaged her wrists.

"Look at that," he murmured, taking her hand in his. "The skin's all red." He leaned down to place a kiss on the side of her wrist where it had chafed the worst. His lips made her heart beat faster. Then he glanced up. "I should have brought a silk scarf, shouldn't I?"

She nodded. He hadn't closed his robe. All that naked skin and his lightly bobbing cock distracted her.

"You didn't get your orgasm."

She agreed with a slow shake of her head.

He unfastened the gag, and she worked her jaw.

"Now was that gag so bad?" he asked in a tone he might use with a child.

"No."

"Would you like your orgasm now?"

"Yes, please."

"Get the vibrator out of my case."

He had a vibrator in there? What had the TSA people thought when they ran his bag through the scanner? Maybe they couldn't identify what it was.

Legs out, he leaned back against the end of the bed and patted his lap. "Sit here."

He was going to watch up close and person as she got herself off?

"Yes, Mr. Sutton." Her voice was anything but meek.

He smiled at that. "Don't tempt me to spank you again." He eyed her. "Or perhaps you'd like to skip the orgasm altogether."

"No, Mr. Sutton." She climbed over him, resting her hips close, his cock feeling heavenly between her legs. She'd teased him with that slit in her skirt, and she'd certainly gotten her payback tonight. She'd enjoyed the spanking and adored the feel of his cock in her mouth, the taste of his come down her throat. But now she wanted him to fuck her. *Please, please.* Begging wouldn't work. But if she was really good with the vibrator, maybe he wouldn't be able to resist. Especially in this position.

He cupped her buttocks in his palms and helped her rise slightly. "Put in the vibrator."

"But—" She stopped. She didn't want to say she was rarely able to climax that way. She'd usually had clitoral orgasms.

He raised one brow at her obvious questioning of his command. "Put. It. In," he stressed.

She rose higher, inserted the vibrator, then slid down until it was fully seated. His cock stood tall against his belly. If she moved slightly, she could rub herself against his shaft.

"I'll hold it while you ride." His gaze seemed to impale her. He squeezed her butt cheeks, then slipped around the front to take control the vibrator. Twisting the base, he turned it on, increasing the speed slowly to full.

Monica licked her lips. It did feel good, perhaps because she had male flesh between her legs as well as his chest so close, the scent of sex rising between them, and his taste lingering in her mouth.

She started to pump on the vibrator, up, down, up, down.

"Slowly," he directed. "Now lean back, anchor yourself on my thighs."

It seemed awkward, but she followed his one and only rule. *Do everything I say.*

Then she gasped. "Oh my God."

He smiled wickedly. Knowingly. Braced on his thighs, the position and the slow pace activated an amazing spot.

"Oh God. How did I not know about this?"

"Because your previous lovers sucked?" he queried blandly.

"Don't be mean." But certainly none of them had found this particular place. Maybe she'd never reached the right level of comfort with any of them in order to experiment.

Which implied she'd found it with Mr. Sutton. Well, she

had fantasized about him for five years. And *he'd* had a lot of women. He must have learned *something*.

"Slow and easy, baby. Ride the G-spot."

Of course. That's what it was. How stupid. She felt gauche. Then he put his finger on her clitoris, and she didn't feel anything but the pleasure.

"Yes-yes-yes," she began to chant.

Her legs quivered. Her breath puffed. She wanted to look at him, but her eyes just seemed to close and her head fell back. There was nothing but the feel of his skin against hers, the circling of his finger, and that spot inside. Oh God, what would it feel like if it was his cock in her?

He bent over her, taking her nipple in his mouth. And bit down. She cried out as sensation streaked to her core. The orgasm ripped through her, more intense than anything she'd ever had on her own.

She gripped him hard with her legs, dug her fingernails into the skin of his thighs, and bucked on the vibrator as if it were real, as if it were him.

The next time, she vowed it *would* be him.

⁂

Her skin flushed a deep rose. Her nipples pearled into tight peaks. And she rode the joy stick for another minute, her body quaking, limbs quivering, eyes screwed tightly shut. He and the vibrator were simply an instrument in that moment, one and the same.

She was gorgeous in her abandon. He adored the feel of her ass beneath his palm when he spanked her, but this moment had its own beauty, too. He wasn't a sadist, he needed her pleasure as well. And there was the slightest kick under his ribcage that he had been the one to show her the intensity of the G-spot. Forty-nine years old, and he felt like he was her first.

She lay collapsed across his legs, her bottom on his lap, her feet flat on the floor. He still held the vibrator inside her but had turned down the speed.

"Oh my God," she whispered, eyes closed.

"You performed well."

She made a sound, a groan perhaps.

He had the idea of pulling her up onto the bed so he could take her again in the night. But he didn't sleep with his submissives. In the morning, she would be his personal secretary again. That was the way it should be. Even a phenomenal blow job could not be allowed to change their relationship. They each had their respective places to keep.

"Did you arrange for the wake-up call?"

Where one moment she'd been boneless across him, the next, her body became a stiff board. "Of course I did. I always do. I haven't forgotten my job."

"I didn't say you had."

She sat up, looked at him, her hazel eyes almost brown in the light of the bedside lamp. "But you've never *reminded* me before."

He was naked except for the robe, while she straddled his bare cock. The vibrator buzzed lightly inside her. He could smell the hot aroma of her come, and his fingers were moist from her orgasm.

Yet the distance was suddenly as wide as the span of the Golden Gate.

She glared. "Do you think too many orgasms are rotting my brain?"

"I don't believe so or my brain would have long since rotted."

"Then why are you asking me?"

"Polite conversation?"

She narrowed her eyes, opened her mouth, shut it again without saying anything. Until finally her nostrils flared slightly and she said, "What is your next order, Mr. Sutton?"

Ah. She was miffed because he interjected business into their intimate act. He might want to order her into his bed, but it wasn't a good idea. They needed to maintain the lines. That blow job had been too good. He could get used to it.

It could warp his sense of authority and control. Not to mention that touch of jealousy he'd felt regarding Kenton. He'd used it to advantage and instigated a superlative punishment session. But things had gotten out of hand.

"We've got an early flight," he said. "You need your rest."

What he really wanted to do was turn the vibrator on high and make her come again. He'd liked that too much as well. He didn't generally hand out orgasms without administering proper punishment at the same time. Women tended to take advantage when they thought they had something a man needed. He'd learned that with his wives.

Her lips thinned. Then she braced herself on his shoulders and pushed off.

For a moment, her delectable pussy was right before his face. He could flick his tongue out to taste her. The urge was so strong that his hands rose to grab her ass and pull her to him.

If she hadn't moved so quickly, he would have done it.

"I ordered your usual coffee, toast, and juice to be delivered at five. The wake-up call will come in at four-thirty. We'll be back in San Francisco shortly after nine West Coast time," she finished, then stalked to the door, closing it loudly behind her.

Despite the gag and the bindings, the blow job had been a mistake. It had been far too good, and that had weakened him into giving her the vibrator orgasm. He should have sent her to her room and told her to finish herself off. But he'd wanted to see her face when she came. She was a goddess when she came. Christ, she'd been a goddess when she was down on her knees with his cock in the ring.

He had to stop thinking of her as a goddess. He'd thought of his first wife that way and look what happened. No, Monica Dawson needed to be kept in her place.

Yet at two in the morning, he woke with his cock hard and dreams of her setting his body on fire. He rose from the bed and padded to the connecting door, telling himself that as her master, it was his right, even his duty, to take what he wanted exactly when he wanted it. *That* would be putting her in her place.

But when he tried the door, she'd locked him out.

CHAPTER ELEVEN

Mr. Sutton had been all business from the moment they met outside their respective hotel rooms. During the taxi ride to the airport, he'd checked his messages on his smart phone and rattled off a list of tasks for her. She'd obediently entered them into her tablet. In the lounge at the airport, he made his calls. Breakfast on the plane was eaten in silence. He even made her sit by the window, forcing her to scramble past him every time she needed to get out of her seat.

The evening had all been so perfect. Why had she ruined everything by locking the door? Who knew what wondrous things might have occurred?

"Would you like another mimosa, sir?" the air hostess asked.

A pretty blonde, she'd been eyeing Mr. Sutton since they'd boarded in Chicago. Perhaps that was why Monica got the window seat, so he could flirt with the woman, whose voice was saccharine sweet. She probably saw a potential sugar daddy. Mr. Sutton had been sappy, smiling at her, effusive over her service, sickeningly polite. He was never *that* polite.

"If I have another, my dear, I'll have to lean on you just

to make it down the gangway."

"Then I better fix you two right away." The woman tittered, actually *tittered*.

Gag me. Monica resisted rolling her eyes. It would have been too obvious. As for her service from the woman, Monica had received cold food, apple juice that tasted winey, and flat lips when she'd requested a replacement.

Mr. Sutton seemed to be enjoying it all. Damn him. Monica wondered if she should tell the poor girl that the most she'd get out of him was a flogging. That would have had her running, instead of sashaying her pert little ass up the center aisle to the first-class galley, his tray in hand. She hadn't even bothered with Monica's.

Obviously Monica was economy class.

Mr. Sutton dug a report out of his briefcase and began reading.

The first-class cabin was filled primarily with businessman types. And two businesswomen. The couple in the front looked like honeymooners from the way they were holding hands, their heads together, a blanket over both their laps. Besides Mr. Sutton, they were the only ones who'd rated extra care from the blonde.

Five minutes later, she returned, putting her hand on Mr. Sutton's shoulder. "Are you *sure* I can't get you that mimosa?" She fluttered her eyelashes. "Or anything else?"

She was *so* obvious. Monica smiled after her boss's second polite *no* and said, "You can take away my tray, thank you very much."

The woman looked at Monica like she was an annoying fly buzzing too close to Mr. Sutton's head.

"Yes, please"—he never said *please* to Monica—"I've got some work I need her to do." He didn't pass the tray but instead let the woman lean over him, her breasts practically poking his eye out. Then he watched that wiggle-walk again, leaning slightly into the aisle to do so.

He'd put Monica in her place and gotten a literal eyeful at the same time. Bastard.

He was punishing her for locking the door. She was his plaything, his submissive, his slave, and she'd locked him out. Rather than ordering her to open up, he was letting her stew today. She'd like the flogging better. She liked the O-ring gag even more. She'd loved having him in her mouth. It was power. It was good. It was sweet victory.

She should have known he'd slam her down. But last night, the way he'd sent her to her room like a plaything he'd tired of, anger—or worse, hurt—had overcome her. She couldn't stand for him to come to her, make her service him. Then walk away again.

She'd wanted to stay in his bed, had been close to begging for the taste of him in her mouth again. She'd wanted to curl into his body, wrap herself around him, lay her head on his chest.

But he'd sent her away, and she'd locked the door. Now she'd never know what would have happened if she'd let him in.

"Monica." His voice was like the sharp edge of a blade.

She sat up straight. "What?" She'd been lost in thought. That wasn't a good thing to do when she was around him. Mr. Sutton demanded attention to detail.

"You're keyed up. You need to relax."

"But I'm." Full-stop. The look he shot her could flay flesh.

He pressed the button for the stewardess. The woman practically tripped on her high heels trying to get to him. "Yes, sir, anything I can do to help you?" She sounded like a good submissive candidate. She should have filled out an application, too. And she once again had her hand on Mr. Sutton's shoulder.

"I'd like a mimosa for my admin." He tipped his head slightly. "We burned the midnight oil." He smiled at the hostess's breasts, which were equally as pert as her ass. "It was a very long night for both of us." He blinked, slowly, letting her get his implied meaning. "She needs a little something to relax with. So heavy on the champagne."

The woman's blue eyes bored into Monica as she saw her sugar-daddy dreams circling the drain. When she returned with the requested drink, he took it from her and handed it to Monica.

"Drink up," he said softly and tipped the glass with his finger on the bottom. There was an intimacy to the gesture. Like the way a man puts his hand on the small of a woman's back, guides her, stakes his claim on her. After one last glare in Monica's direction, the stewardess faded away.

"Don't ever lock your door against me again." His low voice carried a deadly ring.

She gulped the mimosa. The sparkling wine sizzled going down. "No, sir," she whispered.

"When I want you, you are mine. Do you understand?"

"Yes, sir."

"Don't call me sir."

The timber of his voice made her wet. "Yes, Mr. Sutton."

"You deserve punishment." His eyes were dark with intent as he surveyed her.

"Yes, Mr. Sutton." *Please, Mr. Sutton.* She wanted him to take her. She was afraid he'd forever deny her that moment. So instead, she would take him any way she could have him.

That night at home, she didn't tell Sean those thoughts. He would have said she was pathetic. But Sean didn't understand need in the same way she did.

And she needed Mr. Sutton, body and soul.

❦

The work week rolled on, and with each successive day, Rance was increasingly afraid to put his hands on her. Monica Dawson was temptation. She challenged his control. She made him want more than he allowed himself from his submissives. He'd never fucked them simply because he wanted to. And certainly not because he needed to.

But all he could think about was Monica's mouth on him. The memory was exhilarating. His lack of control was debilitating. Even teasing the flight attendant on the plane hadn't alleviated his desire for his sweet Miss Dawson's mouth on his cock.

Brunch with his mother on Thursday—which he'd rescheduled from his usual day due to the West Coast board meeting on Friday—hadn't stopped him thinking about Monica and his cock.

By Friday morning, he still didn't trust himself enough to deliver punishment without succumbing to his need for her. It wouldn't do to allow her to have the upper hand.

This had never happened to him before. Perhaps it was because he'd never chosen a woman like her. His submissives were like his high-maintenance wives. Monica made him want more than simply to dominate her.

He could hear her typing in the outer office. In fifteen minutes, Smythe would arrive to drive them down to Silicon Valley for the monthly board meeting at West Coast. He was chairman. But he wasn't thinking like a chairman now. He was thinking like a man—or a randy teenager—and he wanted her. He wanted to feel her ass under his hand as he delivered a tantalizing spanking. He wanted to feel her climax against his palm. He wanted to taste her. He wanted to bury himself in her.

He was losing his mind.

He punched the intercom button. "Miss Dawson, are you ready to leave?"

"Smythe won't be here for another fifteen minutes." Even her voice through the damn intercom made him hard.

"It will take fifteen minutes just to make it down the elevators at this time of the morning." The office rush hour.

His concentration on business sucked. He never should have picked her as his submissive. Oh wait, he *hadn't* picked her, she'd picked him. She'd been running rings round him from the moment he'd succumbed to her resume.

But Christ, she made him feel alive. His cock pulsed, his

fingers twitched, his nerves tingled, and he could feel every breath in and out of his lungs.

He retrieved his suit jacket. Monica would have the agenda with his notes on it, the monthly financials, everything needed to conduct the meeting. All he had to do was bring his cell phone.

They had to wait for the elevator.

Her navy skirt was tight across her backside, making his hands itch to spank, flog, cup, squeeze, caress, kiss. Her stockings were sheer, her high heels magnificently tall, her nipples tight against the silk of her blouse. She didn't look at him. In the elevator, he detected her scent, that uniquely spicy aroma of arousal. He imagined she wore no panties. The man next to her breathed deeply and cast her a sideways glance. Midthirties, on the good-looking side, fit, blue shirt, black slacks, no tie, he was probably her type. His gaze passed briefly over Rance, and Rance's hands fisted involuntarily. The elevator should have been empty since they were going down. It was the morning, everyone goes up, not down. If they'd been alone, Rance would have shoved Monica up against the wall and tested the panty issue. Damn this man for being here. Damn him for scenting her like he was a hound dog and she was his bitch. Simply damn him.

Rance closed his eyes a moment as they descended. Despite the sense of losing control, this overwhelming awareness felt good. Sexual. Alive. Desire seemed to pump through his veins.

The elevator came to a stop with a slight lurch as they reached the lobby. The young man held out his hand for Monica to precede him, then followed her, cutting Rance off. The queue outside parted for them. Beyond the small crowd, Monica stepped aside, waiting for Rance. The man's eyes roved over her lingeringly.

She didn't seem to notice. Her gaze was on Rance. Her lack of acknowledgment actually puffed him up.

Yes, he *was* losing his mind. But Christ, she was

something to look at.

Rance took her arm to escort her across the lobby to the glass doors, bypassing office workers. Smythe was early, already waiting at the curb. He stood by the open car door as Rance guided Monica, then slid in beside her.

He retrieved his phone from his pocket as soon as Smythe had slipped on his sunglasses, stuck in his earbuds, and pulled into traffic. It would take them ten minutes or longer to reach the freeway despite the fact that it was only a few blocks. That was San Francisco's financial district, always humming.

After settling her briefcase and purse at her feet, Monica sighed softly—she probably thought he couldn't hear—and looked out the window.

Rance keyed a text and pressed Send. Seconds later, her phone chirped. She reached into her bag, sat back, then touched the screen and read. She looked at him, then back to the message, then to him once more.

He didn't move a muscle. He merely waited.

Her lips parted as if she might protest.

He raised a brow.

Setting her phone on the seat between them, she began to raise her skirt.

His heart thumped against his chest in a fast rhythm. Her skin was smooth beneath the sheer stocking. Every inch of thigh was tempting enough to nibble. Her gaze flitted up to the rearview mirror. Rance noted that Smythe appeared to be concentrating on the road, the lights, the traffic weaving in and out as he maneuvered the car safely to their destination.

The skirt reached the lacy tops of her thigh-highs. Rance held his breath. He wanted to sink his teeth into that tasty flesh. Wanted to bury his face against her, drink in her scent.

They entered the freeway, Smythe merging with the traffic coming from all directions.

Monica lifted her hips slightly and raised the skirt to reveal moist pink flesh. His breath was trapped in his lungs.

His heart stopped beating. She was trimmed but not bare. And she was wet. He could smell it, see it, damn near taste it.

He keyed in another message. Texting was somehow sexier than giving her a voice command. Her phone trilled on the seat between them. Smythe's head turned infinitesimally, as if the sound had penetrated his earbuds, then he went back to the road, facing straight ahead, his eyes masked by the dark sunglasses. In the rearview, he would be able to see Monica only from the chest up. And since she was seated behind him, he couldn't turn to look at her.

Monica tapped the screen and read the message without even picking up the phone.

Her breath hitched.

Rance's did, too.

She looked at him. He tipped his head.

Then she did what he'd ordered her to do.

∽

Touch yourself for me.

Monica was utterly creamy, had been from the moment she read that first text telling her to pull up her skirt.

How did he do that? He'd ignored her all week, yet her heart went into overdrive the moment he gave her the slightest bit of attention. She'd even given herself several orgasms every night, following his instructions to the letter.

She'd barely spoken to Sean this week. If she had, everything would have poured out. She couldn't tell him. He'd call her all kinds of an idiot for getting her emotions entangled.

She might very well be stupid, but she was Mr. Sutton's submissive and subject to his whims. She'd agreed to it for the prescribed period, and they had weeks to go on the arrangement. And she wouldn't miss a single moment of her two months.

He looked at her. Was he breathing hard? His buttoned

suit jacket hid anything that might be going on in his pants. Yet there was an avid light in his eyes.

She slid between her slippery folds. He'd told her to touch herself, and she was going for the gusto. The most Smythe would see was hand movement. Though her face might give her away. Whatever. Her master had made spoken.

She stroked the button of her clitoris. Almost without intention, she slouched down slightly in the seat. Her body began to hum. She moaned. Smythe wouldn't hear. But if she bit her lip to keep it in, he'd notice. Not that it mattered. Surely he'd known Mr. Sutton had put his hand between her legs during that shopping trip last week.

Sensation built, spread out, from her clitoris, up her arms, down her legs, deep into her belly. Mr. Sutton's gaze devoured her and made everything hotter. God, she loved to be watched. She loved it when *he* watched her. It had been so long, not since Monday, days and days ago.

Her head fell back against the seat. Her eyes closed. Her hips undulated against her touch.

Then her phone twittered, the short burst of sound signaling another message. Even the texting was hot. No words, just the screen, just his gaze confirming the dirty messages. She didn't stop her rhythm, lifting the phone to tap the screen with her thumb to read.

Make yourself come for me.

She looked at him, reading his eyes as easily as if he'd spoken. *Do it now.*

She allowed her hips to roll, meeting the stroke of her fingers, intensifying the friction. A sigh slipped from her mouth, then a groan. Every nerve was on fire. She circled faster, harder, slipping, sliding, soaring. Her body clenched, and she curled down, clamping her hand between her legs. A series of jolts electrified her. She pressed her thighs hard, riding out the climax. Until finally she flopped back against the seat again, breathing hard, her body suddenly boneless.

Then the phone chirped again.

She didn't shimmy her skirt down. She sat exposed before him and read his next missive.

Rub your lips then lick your fingers.

Her taste was slightly salty yet somehow sweet as well.

He texted again.

Now kiss me. I want to taste you.

Her heart literally stopped beating. He hadn't kissed her. He'd done all manner of things to her, but he hadn't kissed her yet.

Monica swept over to his side of the car and put her mouth on his. She gave him her lips, her tongue, her soul. He took everything, slicking her mouth with his tongue. He consumed her, angling his lips across hers and going deep. All without putting his hands on her. It was hot, it was fast, it was devastating. And it left her the same way as always, needing so much more.

CHAPTER TWELVE

Rance was hard all day. And it was fucking good.

The board room was full. Monica sat along the back wall, taking notes as usual. The financials were discussed, new product releases detailed, machine upgrades signed off on, carafes of coffee drunk, and sandwiches eaten. The VPs trooped in for their reports. Everything was routine.

In stray moments, his attention wandered briefly, very briefly, to those minutes in the car.

He hadn't succumbed to her allure. He'd been her master, getting her to do dirty things she would never before have dreamed of doing in front of his driver.

The kiss had been nothing more than a reward. He'd steeped himself in her sweetness for only a few moments. She'd tasted minty, delicious, her lips softening under his command, his tongue taking hers. Of course, the kiss was more about her needs than his own, something a submissive desired after a performance. He didn't usually think about that—in fact, he avoided it—but he'd given her a little tenderness today. He should have offered it on Monday night. Then she wouldn't have locked the door. She was different from his other women. She needed more. She'd performed well and followed his instructions, and he'd rewarded her. That's all he'd done, dole out a little tenderness as a reward.

"Will you have dinner this evening with the executive team?" Holt Montgomery asked after the meeting had drawn to a close.

Montgomery was West Coast's CEO. He kept a stern hand on the workings of the company, and it had thrived under his command. The man was sharp but he was fair. Probably his only weakness was his secretary, Ruby Williams. He'd gotten too involved, to the point where he was actually marrying the woman at the end of next month.

You didn't marry your secretary. You didn't fall in love with your submissive.

But who was Rance to judge another man's personal choices as long as they didn't affect any professional decisions? He'd given his blessing to the union at the previous board meeting.

He followed Montgomery into the hallway outside the boardroom. Monica had dashed off to the restroom to powder her nose or some such thing.

"A special occasion?" Since all the members were from the Bay Area, they didn't normally have a dinner after a meeting. It also didn't appear that the rest of the board was invited.

Montgomery unbuttoned his suit jacket, now that the formal presentations were over. "An engagement party, of sorts. Of all the board members, you and I have worked together the longest. Ruby and I would be honored to have you attend."

"Of course," he agreed. A little camaraderie never hurt a business relationship.

"I've booked at Scopponi's in downtown Palo Alto." The classy seafood place was only a short distance. Montgomery glanced at his watch. "Six o'clock."

That was early for the dinner hour, but Rance wouldn't have to cool his heels for an extended period. "Good. It will give us a chance to talk about your staff. You really do need to consider adding a qualified woman." He didn't want to see the company lambasted for being out of step with the times.

"My thought also," Holt said. "Clay and I have had discussions about promoting our Human Resources director. We both feel that with the current headcount and the projected growth for next year the executive staff will benefit from a vice president of HR. It could be construed as a conflict of interest to have HR reporting to the CFO."

"Good thinking." Rance slapped him lightly on the arm.

"Of course, Miss Dawson is included in the invitation dinner."

Ah, Miss Dawson. "I'm sure she'll be delighted." He didn't insult Montgomery by asking if the company was footing the bill for this little get-together. If he'd call it an engagement party, Montgomery would not be stiffing West Coast. In addition to the other qualities which made him an exceptional leader, he had integrity. "Thank you," Rance concluded.

Monica didn't generally attend social functions after their work day was over. Even when traveling, she preferred to eat on her own, citing the fact that it wasn't right to charge the corporation's expense account. He'd taught her well. Besides, his obligations weren't hers. He'd also had the sense that once the meetings were over, she simply wanted time on her own.

At least she had until she'd become his submissive.

She would attend tonight because he willed it. He wasn't sending her back up to San Francisco on her own. She was his. From now on, no skipping out on dinners or functions. He liked the idea of having her beside him. He could touch her under the table, demonstrate his ownership. If he chose. Because he was the one in control.

Yes, he'd been fucking hard all day. And it was so damn good.

⊙≈≈⊙

Monica had met all these people at one time or another. So she couldn't say why she felt out of place. Maybe her feelings were still skewed by that episode in Mr. Sutton's car. His sexting. His kiss. She'd been off balance since this morning.

Holt Montgomery held the seat at the head of the table. In his early fifties, with thick, steel-gray hair, his bearing reminded her of Mr. Sutton. They both wore authority like a second skin. She had to admit to feeling a few tingles of awareness over the years. She'd always liked older men. But Mr. Sutton stood apart from them all by a mile.

"To my beautiful bride." Holt raised his wineglass to Ruby Williams, who was seated on his left, and the group followed suit. On the same side of the table, Monica couldn't see Ruby or her reaction, but it probably wasn't a blush. Monica had the feeling Ruby Williams hadn't blushed since she was thirteen. It was funny how much you picked up just by watching people. And seated behind everyone in all the meetings, Monica had done a lot of watching.

She'd chosen a champagne cocktail for the toast, and the cool sparkling liquid sent a fizz through her veins. There was clapping and good wishes.

There were twelve in attendance, including wives or girlfriends. Neal Thomas and David Farris were the only two without a date. David's wife had died of cancer last year, poor man. Monica had, however, seen him in the hall once with the new Finance manager, Tricia Connelly. She'd gotten a feeling. They'd stood a tad too close, David's expression a little too intense. Monica's radar had picked up something, though she wasn't sure what. Neal Thomas was married, but his wife was absent. Monica thought that a little odd since the celebration had seemed almost compulsory.

She was seated next to Mr. Sutton, who'd been given the opposite end of the table from Holt over which to preside. They didn't occupy a different room in the restaurant, but they were in the back with a banquette separating them from the rest of the diners. Tables had been pushed together and covered with white cloths. They were served by two dedicated waiters, a man and a woman, and their own busboy who kept the water glasses topped and the bread basket full. The scent of garlic and white wine sauce permeated the air. Monica had chosen the shrimp scampi.

Even more delicious that the scampi was the fact that she could move her knee and encounter Mr. Sutton's leg under the table. Would anyone notice if she put her hand on him?

"So, Miss Dawson, do you enjoy the travel you're able to do with Mr. Sutton?" Neal Thomas was seated across from her.

With a spurt of guilt, she curled her hands in her lap.

"Please, call me Rance," Mr. Sutton said. "And I'm sure Monica would prefer you use her first name as well."

She noted a look pass between Ward Restin and Spencer Benedict and wondered at the glance they both shot her way.

Neal continued. "Of course. Monica." West Coast's VP of Business Development had thick black hair, which he wore a little too long, and with his penetrating blue eyes, he was quite attractive. Despite the fact that he was Mr. Sutton's age, she couldn't detect any gray.

"The trips are usually quick," she told him. "We're on the go the whole time. So I wouldn't necessarily call it *travel*."

Mr. Sutton chuckled. "I'll have to give you more time for sightseeing, Monica."

Monica. There was something in the way he said it that made her heart flutter. She was always Miss Dawson. Even when he was spanking her. Or watching her ride a vibrator. Something sparked in Mr. Sutton's eyes as if he'd read her thoughts.

Spence Benedict and Ward Restin were studying her again. As if *they* had an inkling, too. They were making her nervous, and she was glad when the conversation turned to some of the unique features of different American cities.

VP of R&D, Ward Restin was the most bookish of the

lot of them, with wire-rimmed glasses and short brown hair. How on earth he'd ended up with Holt Montgomery's daughter, Cassandra, Monica couldn't even begin to guess. Monica had met her only once before, when they'd been in the lobby after a board meeting. Cassandra had flitted through to see her father. She was flamboyant, with curly red hair that looked like something out of a classic painting. She obviously adored the bespectacled man, leaning in close as he spoke. She could have been touching him under the table.

Spence Benedict was the marketing man. The job suited him. She'd always thought he was a little slick. Which is why his girlfriend Zoe Hudson was such a surprise. She seemed sweet, with lovely black hair she'd wound up into a knot on her head. Her hand was clasped in Spence's on the table. Monica felt an unexpected ache at the sight.

She wasn't comfortable with any of them really. She felt like the amoeba swimming around on the slide under their microscope. Maybe that was because she'd never spoken to them except in an entirely business sense.

Holt tapped his wineglass with a fork, and conversation ceased.

"I have an announcement." His voice was a deep baritone. "Actually, it's Clay's news." He made a flourish to turn the attention over to Clay Blackwell.

Clay didn't stand, but she knew he was well over six feet. A handsome man with short dark hair, he laid his arm across the seat back of the woman next to him. Jessica Murphy, blond-haired and blue-eyed in contrast to Clay's darkness, had been West Coast's Accounting manager until a few months ago. Clay had also been Ruby Williams' live-in lover, an arrangement that ended at the same time Jessica left the company. It was no secret the two events were related.

"Jessica and I are leaving for Tahoe in the morning. We're getting married."

There were cheers all around, just has there had been for Holt and Ruby. But there were also swift looks passing every which way, a whole lot of them centering on Ruby. Under other circumstances, Clay probably would have made some sort of speech, but with Ruby right there, Monica suspected he didn't want to make a bigger deal than Holt already had. Seated on the same side of the table, Monica couldn't see Ruby's expression, and it would have been rude to lean forward for a look. The woman was marrying Holt anyway, so why would she care?

Monica glanced at Mr. Sutton. He met her eyes as if he'd been watching her all along.

"Are the boys going to be witnesses for you?" Holt asked into the celebratory noise.

Clay had two sons in high school. "They heartily approve, but we're going on our own. We'll celebrate with the boys when we get back." He looked at Jessica with a melting gaze that gave Monica's heart a lurch much the same as Zoe Hudson's hand locked in Spence's had. She couldn't look at Mr. Sutton—who was still Mr. Sutton to her, never Rance.

Holt grinned and rapped the table with his knuckles. "Take Monday off and spend an extra day in Tahoe since it's your honeymoon."

Clay returned the grin and nodded. Holt sat and individual conversations began again around the table. The wait staff returned to clear the dinner plates in preparation for dessert.

Ruby stood, and Monica heard something about the women's room. Holt pushed his chair back, too, and followed. This was as good a time as any for a bathroom break, and Monica excused herself also.

Before she could rise, though, Mr. Sutton circled her wrist, pulling her close until his lips were at her ear. "Touch yourself while you're in there. I want to think of that while I'm waiting for you to return."

A shiver passed through her. He made everything sexual. Sensual. Even a dinner party with ten other guests. But he didn't make it adoring.

Ruby and Holt had already disappeared by the time she followed their example. A sign directed her down a hallway, and she was just about to turn a corner when she heard voices.

Monica froze against the wall. Holt and Ruby hadn't gone into the restrooms.

"Why didn't you tell me?" Ruby's voice was a low hiss of anger.

"Because Clay told me just before I walked in. Did you want me to blurt it out in front of everyone?" A thread of exasperation tinged Holt's words.

"You *did* blurt it out in front of everyone," she accused.

"You know what I meant." He gave a long-suffering male sigh.

"That bitch stole my thunder. This was *my* night."

"It's still your night, Ruby."

Monica knew she should have returned to the dining room. Anyone could walk back here and discover her eavesdropping.

Holt went on, his voice low but harsh. "May I remind you that you're marrying *me* in a little over a month? Whatever Clay and Jessica do has nothing to do with us."

"You're such a man," she snapped. "I'm not jealous. It's about being the center of attention."

Ruby Williams was always the center of attention, even when she was quietly filling the coffee carafe during a board meeting.

"If you're not careful, you'll be getting some extra attention tonight." There was a change in Holt's voice, huskier, darker. Dirtier.

Monica felt herself heat at the implied *something*.

"Don't you dare," Ruby said in a seductive tone that totally dared him.

"Behave yourself or you're going to feel the flat of my hand on that pretty ass of yours." He paused. Or maybe he was touching her. "While your hands are tied behind your back." Another pause interrupted only by a light sound that could have been a female groan. "And a gag in your hot little mouth. Until I'm ready for you to use your lips on me."

Monica put her hand up to hold in the gasp. Spanking? A gag? Tied up? Her cheeks flushed. She was afraid they'd hear her breathe. Except that they seemed far too involved in their own conversation and whatever Holt was doing.

This time, she definitely heard Ruby moan.

"Jesus, I could fuck you right here." Monica strained to catch each one of Holt's words.

"God, yes."

Ruby's answer set her on fire. All Monica could think about was getting back to Mr. Sutton. Touching Mr. Sutton. Pleasing Mr. Sutton.

❧

Well, that had been quite some *touching herself* Monica had done on her trip to the ladies' room. She'd returned with flushed cheeks, rapid breathing, and the sweet scent of arousal perfuming the air around her. Rance had noted a similar reaction in Ruby and the satisfied smile on Holt's face upon their return. It didn't take a lot of speculation to figure things out. Rance's conjecture only served to heighten his desires.

His cock was hard and at the ready in anticipation of the drive back to San Francisco. Cocooned with Monica in the car, her scent would turn him mad with need.

He hatched a plan as they ate dessert and drank coffee, while she damn near panted in her seat. He refined the plan as they said their goodbyes and offered congratulations to the bride and groom of tomorrow. He began the plan's execution as Smythe pulled up in front of the restaurant and Rance helped Monica into the car. He stroked the soft skin of her upper arm, let his fingers trail down, kept her hand in his as he followed her into the backseat.

Undoing his suit jacket with one hand, he let her palm graze the hard ridge of his cock before Smythe climbed into the front seat.

"I received a text message that your corsets are ready."

She blinked, then shook her head as if the gesture would give his words sense. She'd been functioning in a haze of need and desire, and his statement obviously threw her off.

"I'll have Smythe pick you up at ten tomorrow morning and take you to pick them up."

She pressed her lips together, clearly annoyed once she understood that he wasn't going to touch her. Or ask her to touch him. "I'm perfectly capable of getting over there by myself."

"I said Smythe will drive you. And you should get lessons on how to lace them properly."

"The girl already showed me how to lace them." Her voice was slightly waspish.

He smiled. He liked her a little miffed. Because soon he'd turn the tables again. "Do as I say," he said softly but sternly.

"Yes, Mr. Sutton." She simpered.

Christ, it made him hot. When Smythe hit the freeway and headed north, Rance turned in his seat so that he was nestled in the corner and crooked one knee. The spread of his legs defined the bulge of his cock. Her gaze dropped to the sight. Her breathing kicked up to a faster pace.

Retrieving his phone from his jacket pocket, he began a text. A few seconds after he pressed Send, her cell chirped. She reached in her purse, tapped the screen.

She bit her lip but didn't look at him. Not yet. Then she couldn't resist licking her lips. It was all the answer he needed.

You want my cock in your mouth, don't you?

Yes, she wanted it bad.

When she didn't type a reply, he sent her a second text and watched her read it. *My cock is so fucking hard. I've been thinking about you making yourself come in the restroom.*

He dropped a hand to his pants and stroked himself through the material.

Her lips parted. She drew in a shaky breath. Then she swallowed, and he knew she was remembering the taste of his come.

He typed again and waited for her reaction. *I'm going to jack off tonight thinking about shoving my cock deep into your mouth.*

This time her eyes widened. Even in the dimness of the car along the freeway, he could see her pupils darken. The muscles along her jaw were tight with the grinding of her teeth.

He was a tease. The question was written all over her features. Why didn't he let her do it now? Why didn't he take her home and make her do it there? Why, why, why?

Poor Miss Dawson. He desired her, but he also controlled her. He controlled himself. And he could prove it by waiting. A man who didn't have control would already have succumbed, especially considering the ache in his balls. But Rance Sutton was completely controlled.

He put the phone in his pocket.

"We have a date tomorrow night," he told her.

She didn't speak, her lips thinning mutinously.

"Smythe will pick you up at nine. I want you to wear the red corset. You should choose a black skirt to go with it." He frowned a moment in consideration. "That flared one you usually wear with the teal waistcoat and cream-colored blouse."

She watched him steadily. She hadn't said a word since her last *Yes, Mr. Sutton.* All she'd done was throw eye daggers at him. That made him hard, too. Everything she did excited him.

"Thigh-high stockings, no panties, and your black suede heels," he concluded. Then he raised one brow.

"Yes, Mr. Sutton." She didn't ask him where they'd be going.

Should he tell her? Definitely. He wanted her to think about it for the next twenty-four hours. Anticipate it. Fear it.

"We're attending a BDSM club. You will see all manner

of debauchery. Floggings, spankings, restraints, humiliation. You will see sex. Men with women, men with men, women with women. Ménages. Gang bangs."

The haughty anger fled. Her eyes filled with dread. Her lips quivered. He imagined she was ready to beg. And he gave her what she feared.

"I expect you to perform for our audience." He lowered his voice to a deadly note. "Anything I tell you to do, anytime, anywhere."

When Smythe let her out of the car, she ran and didn't look back.

Rance had damn near come in his pants. When he got home, he'd finish what she'd started.

And tomorrow night, she would be at his mercy.

CHAPTER THIRTEEN

Too wrapped up in preparing for his own sizzling date with hot-and-cold Jim, Sean hadn't hounded her as she got ready. In fact, he hadn't crawled into her bed this week and asked for the latest update either. He'd been busy seducing Jim into coming out.

Tonight, as she entered the living, he was dressed to the nines in a tux.

"Oh my God." She gaped. "You're totally hot. Even I'd do you." If he was Mr. Sutton.

He fanned his face. "Tickets to the symphony. I sprang for a private box."

"Wow. Big spender."

Sean rolled his eyes dramatically. "Jim assures me it's not a date. He says he just loves the symphony and can't pass it up."

"You're so devious. But you hate the symphony."

"Who cares? Believe me, he's not going to object one eensy-teensy bit if I drop down below the parapet and suck him off to the cannons firing in the 1812 Overture."

"Are they using real cannons?" she asked.

This time the eye roll and sigh were for her. "And look at you. That corset is sexy as hell. Another present from

Master?"

She smoothed her hand over the red satin. She'd even managed to lace it as tight as the shop girl had, so that it held her back straight and plumped her breasts.

Sean eyed her critically. "I like the skirt, but you should wear something short, tight, and leather.

"He told me to wear this one." She pointed down. "And these shoes." It had come as a surprise that Mr. Sutton actually catalogued her wardrobe. She was sure she hadn't worn this skirt since signing her contract with him. That meant he'd been noticing her for quite some time.

"Definitely a pretty pair of fuck-me heels, sweetie. Where's he taking you?"

"He didn't tell me." She wasn't going to mention the BDSM club. In fact, she'd been trying not to think about that part of the evening. Floggings and sex, men with men, even gang bangs. Plus he expected *her* to perform. What had terrified her as she lay in bed last night was *how* she'd have to perform. Yet despite the fear, she'd come hard and long, a barrage of images flooding her mind. She'd never watched anyone have sex. The idea was titillating. And man on man was downright arousing.

"Not knowing what he's going to do is even hotter." Sean approved, shooting out his wrist to raise the cuff and reveal his watch. "I better get going before my Cinderella changes his mind." He pecked Monica on the cheek. "Let's swap stories tonight," he whispered in her ear.

He was gone without waiting for an answer. Which was good since she didn't have one.

In the kitchen, she poured herself a glass of wine. A little something for her nerves. She was all pins and needles. Was Smythe taking her to meet Mr. Sutton at the club? Would she have to enter the place on her own? She didn't even know where it was. Not knowing made her nerve endings jangle.

Was this what submission was all about? Accepting the unexpected? Leaving everything up to the whim of her master? In the privacy of her own kitchen, she could admit she didn't want a club scene. She didn't want to be exposed or humiliated. She'd wanted this affair to be just the two of them. But she'd signed away all her rights when she'd put her signature on that contract. She wasn't sure she was getting what she'd hoped for.

What if he let another man flog her? What if he made her have sex with someone else? God, what if *he* had sex with another woman? That would kill her. She didn't even have a safe word because he'd said she wouldn't need one.

The wine wasn't helping like she'd thought it would. Her nerves were strung so tightly she could almost feel them pop inside her. She checked her makeup in a nervous gesture. Her lipstick should remain intact for the night since she'd used a long-lasting type that didn't wear off.

She startled when the doorbell rang, then glanced at her watch. Oh my God. She was late. She should have been waiting downstairs for Smythe. Thank goodness Sean had already left or she would have been busted.

She hadn't even arrived at the club and the night was already going downhill.

The club was in the Tenderloin, not the sweetest part of San Francisco. The sidewalks were broken, people congregated in doorways, shuffled between parked vehicles, and cop cars sat on every corner. The odd thing was that all you had to do was cross Mason and you were almost at Powell, with the cable car turnaround, the Westfield shopping center across Market, and Union Square up the street. A tourist mecca.

As for the club itself, a big bruiser stood at the door keeping the riffraff out. Once inside, Rance would protect her. A car rolled to a stop curbside, and Smythe stepped out. He opened the door, then Rance took over, holding out his hand.

Monica's fingers trembled in his. He stood for a moment with her on the sidewalk as he rattled off instructions to Smythe. "I'll call you when we're ready. Text me when you arrive, and we'll come down."

"Yes, sir," Smythe said, his hand moving upwards as if he might actually salute.

In his hand, Monica's fingers finally relaxed. At least a little. She carried a small clutch purse, and at the door they each surrendered their license for a brief inspection.

The outer entry led into a wide hall at the foot of a long staircase, and they left the stench of the street behind them with the snick of the closing door. The contrast was what Rance liked about this place, the seedy neighborhood outside, the opulence of textured walls and lushly carpeted stairs to lead them up.

He held out their clasped hands. "The corset is perfect." She was magnificent.

"Thank you," she murmured.

The color on her lush lips matched the deep red tones of the satin. The tight lacing pushed up her gorgeous breasts just short of revealing the cherry sweetness of her nipples. Her hourglass figure was accentuated, the corset flaring slightly over her hips. His heart beat faster as he imagined wrapping his hands around her waist and taking her from behind. He had plans for that flirty little skirt, too. Had she worn panties with the thigh-highs? He couldn't remember if he'd specified, but he liked the anticipation hardening his cock as he considered several scenarios. And those shoes, Christ, her legs seemed endless. How many times had his cock stirred as he'd watched her stride from his office? More times than he'd even been aware.

"You follow directions to the letter," he complimented her.

He held her hand as they climbed the wide staircase, her heels sinking into the plush carpet. The reception desk at the top resembled something in a classy beauty salon, all white and glass and chrome.

He didn't bother to flash his membership card.

"Ah, Mr. Sutton, it's so good to see you again." The husky voice emerged from a classically beautiful woman at the desk. Her café au lait skin was rouged, her eyelids shadowed in purple. The tight Lycra tank molded to breasts that were barely more than a mouthful, and her short leather skirt stopped halfway down her well-formed thighs. Around her throat, she wore a studded collar. It disguised the protruding Adam's apple that would give her away, if her deep voice hadn't already done so.

Rance smiled. Once again, it was the contrasts that appealed to him. Cross-dresser transgender, it was all part of the landscape. "I've brought a new lady with me tonight, Dominique." Despite her name, Dominique was not a dom. She was a switch, meaning she could play top or bottom. And enjoyed either position equally.

"Your friends are always welcome. We just need her to sign our guest protocol." Dominique slid over a clipboard and pen.

Monica bit her lip, glanced at Rance, then began reading the one-page document. It listed a few simple rules. Don't bother people. Don't get creepy. No means no. Negotiate the scene you want to play in advance. Spectators are welcome on the dungeon floor, but no talking unless you're in play. Condoms required. Clean your fluids off the equipment when you're done.

Her cheeks flushed as she read.

Of course, as his guest, he was required to keep Monica in line. He picked up the pen. "Sign, my dear."

Dominique put her palm over Monica's before she could take the proffered pen. The hair had been waxed from the back of her masculine hand. "Honey, only sign if this is really what you want." Dominique was pushing. Rance didn't mind.

Though Dominique knew him well, it was her job to warn the newbies. Trouble came if they were coerced and didn't understand what they were getting into. Everyone got the speech. Everyone had a choice. Another reason why he liked this club despite the dicey location.

Glancing at Rance, Dominique wrinkled her nose. "Don't let this hunk boss you around." She lowered her voice, which deepened it even more. "Unless you're dying for him to boss you around. It's all about what *you* want."

Monica swallowed hard, then puffed out a breath. "I'd like to sign."

Dominique released her hand. "You'll be safe. He's just a big pussycat anyway." She batted false lashes at him. Rance almost laughed. He'd never been described as a pussycat. He was not known as a fluffy daddy dom who petted and pampered and soothed his submissives. But neither did he make them cry. Except in pleasure.

"I'm not afraid," Monica said, her voice exhibiting more bravado than before.

"Just remember. Our safe word is actually *safe word*. So if anything is happening to you that your really don't want, just yell it out and one of DMs will stop the scene right away."

"That's a dungeon master," Rance supplied.

"We prefer dungeon monitor," Dominique countered.

Monica was getting that wide-eyed look again. His pulse rate rose considering how much was in store for her. He planned to test her limits and give her an experience she'd never forget.

"I won't need the safe word," she said softly. And signed her name. Signed her trust.

No matter the things he'd done or the man he was or what he'd planned for her tonight, she'd still granted him her trust.

He hadn't thought about it at the time she'd signed their contract. It was only now, with Dominique's subtle warnings still lingering, that he felt the impact of Monica's trust. Here and now. In this place, which, to her, must truly be terrifying.

He hadn't considered her motivations. Why did she want to experience his world? What had fascinated her? Whatever her reason, bondage, dominance, submission, and everything they entailed, were still new to her and as frightening as they were exciting. Yet she'd followed him inside this den of inequity.

Rance held out his hand. She placed her palm in his, and he curled his fingers around hers. "I'll take care of her, Dominique. Don't worry."

"No one's ever complained about you, Mr. Sutton." Dominique looked down at Rance's side. "You seem to have forgotten your tool bag. Did you need to borrow anything?"

"Thank you. I'll talk to Laurence when I'm ready." He wouldn't need to speak with Laurence. He had other plans. But he didn't need to reveal them to his sweet Miss Dawson yet.

They stepped into a larger antechamber. While reception was an institutional blue-gray carpet, here, everything was black but no less plush. A long coat rail was already slung with jackets and sweaters. Lockers lined the opposite wall, and restrooms were on either side of the double doors at the end.

The room was empty for the moment. They were late for the first rush, early for the second. "It's not what I expected," she said.

"What did you expect?"

"I…" She closed her mouth, thinking. "I really don't know. Sex everywhere, I guess. This is so"—she flourished a hand—"normal." She pointed to the rail. "You hang up your coat." She tilted her chin at the lockers. "You put your stuff there." At that point, she seemed to remember her small clutch. "What should I do with this?"

He withdrew a combination lock from his pocket. "Do you need anything out of it?"

"No. Not now."

He laid the purse in a locker. "You can always retrieve it when you have a need." He closed the lock and whirled the dial.

Monica splayed a hand. "That's what I'm talking about. It's so civilized. Like you're at the gym."

He laughed. "Believe me, I'm going to give you a workout." Then he shrugged out of his suit jacket and hung it on the rack. Beneath it he wore a shirt and tie. Inside, there would be jeans, chains, leathers, all manner of dress according to the whims of the individual. For tonight, he preferred to be…civilized.

"Are you ready?"

"No," she said honestly, her pretty eyes serious. "But I've always wondered what you do. The logistics. The real thing, I mean. Since it's not like I didn't know you came to these places."

Yes, he'd even had her buy his toys. How perverse. Once again, he had to consider that he'd been setting the stage all along. Drawing her in. He wasn't used to engaging in self-analysis. He simply did what he wanted when he wanted. He didn't delude himself, as far as he knew. He'd always told himself she was too good a secretary to play with. Yet he'd been seducing her with little snippets of his other life.

It was clear his subconscious had intention. Now his intentions were highly conscious.

He tucked her arm through his. "No more guessing, Miss Dawson. Tonight you'll see everything."

Far more than she'd ever bargained for.

❧

She was about to step fully into his world. That's what Monica was afraid of. Up to now, there had been only small windows into his lifestyle. Not that *he* called it a lifestyle. He wouldn't admit to following rules or doing anything the way everyone else did.

But that lady—or man—at the front desk had known him. She offered to let him *borrow* whatever he wanted. *Talk to Laurence.* Mr. Sutton was a regular. He knew everyone. They knew him. He'd brought other women here, the women Monica had purchased sex toys for.

She shuddered. She didn't want to think about that.

"What's a scene?" The question was a stalling tactic. She wasn't sure she was ready for whatever was beyond those doors. This room was too black, black carpet, black walls, black lockers. The only color came from the clothing on the coat rail.

Mr. Sutton tipped his head in question.

"One of the rules," she clarified. "It said to negotiate the scene you want to play in advance."

"We're all acting in order to get what we want. So you negotiate with your prospective partner on how you want to play it." He stroked her arm, from elbow to wrist.

She frowned.

"Maybe you want to play daddy-daughter. Or cop and prisoner. Or maybe you just want to be humiliated, put in a cage, ignored, then dragged out and spanked." He kept touching her as he explained, as if holding her with words wasn't enough. "What do you want? What does your partner want? Can you find a scene that works for both of you?"

"Oh." She bit her lip. "Why didn't we negotiate?"

He drew his finger straight up the front of her corset, between her breasts, and circled her throat with his hand. "Because you're my submissive. I brought you here. You've already agreed to do whatever I want. There is no negotiation. That's just for hookups."

She swallowed beneath his palm. The feel of his hand around her was intoxicating. Like the leather collar the woman at the front desk had worn. His hand made her feel as warm as his compliments had down in the small entry. She wanted to ask how often he'd come here for a hookup. Then just as quickly she didn't want to know.

"That's not my scene," he said.

Damn it, everything was written on her face.

"I choose a woman to work with. The way I chose you."

"You didn't choose me," she whispered, her voice slightly strangled as if his hold on her were tight.

"I always choose," he said. His eyes reflected the black walls of the room. "And I chose you." His mouth was close, so close. His body pressed against her. His hand around her throat owned her. "Are you ready to step inside? You've been stalling long enough."

His voice made her knees weak. "I'm ready." She would never be ready. But this was how she could have him. This was the scene she'd negotiated when she'd signed his contract.

"Then let us begin," he whispered.

CHAPTER FOURTEEN

Mr. Sutton pushed through the double doors, giving Monica no choice but to follow.

Of course, she'd follow him anywhere after those words had melted her insides. *I chose you.*

The locker room, or whatever they called it, opened onto a wide hallway with overstuffed chairs and a couple of sofas lining each side. Through slatted wood blinds on their right, she made out a bar area and more sofa and chair groupings. Noise swelled out from the room, pumping into the wide hall.

Music was playing, some kind of rock, but it wasn't obtrusive. Three separate couples sprawled in the hall chairs. One young woman hugged her girlfriend, stroking her hair, her face, planting kisses and murmuring soft words.

Where was the bondage? And the kinky sex?

"That's the afterglow," Mr. Sutton described the scene. "The dom taking care of her sub after a scene." He shrugged. "I'm not the fluffy daddy type."

She laughed out loud, drawing more than one pair of eyes, and put a hand over her mouth to stifle the rest. "I never imagined that you would be."

Agreeing with a slight smile, he took her elbow and

guided her into the bar. "A drink?"

She wasn't sure she should admit she'd already had a glass of wine at home. But what the heck, a little more would ease her nerves. "White wine."

The music was louder in here. So were the voices. Laughter and shouting, people talking over one another. A table against the far wall was laid out with a spread of chips, salsa, vegetables, and fruit. The crowd was dressed in anything from shredded jeans and tights, miniskirts and short-shorts, Goth black and punk rock, plain old jeans and work shirts to suit and tie like Mr. Sutton. There was even a man wearing a leather hood obscuring his entire face, only his eyes and fleshy lips protruding. The age range was equally as wide. Good lord, some of the girls looked like they were in their early twenties. With multiple piercings.

In a divided room a step up from the main area was a long corner group. And here were the people of Mr. Sutton's ilk. Monica saw evening dresses and sport coats. With two wines in hand, Mr. Sutton raised a glass to an older gentleman. The man saluted in turn and inclined his head.

"Who's that?"

He handed her the wine. "Someone of like mind," he told her. "We have, on occasion, meted out discipline together."

The man was handsome, she had to admit, and well kept. In fact, surveying the group seated there, it was like looking at the West Coast dinner last night.

"So where's all the action?" she murmured. "Do people just sit around and drink and talk?"

He trailed a finger down her cheek. "Impatient to start, are we?"

"No." But her stomach was jumping. It was like waiting for the dentist's needle, but once he started drilling, it wasn't as bad as you thought.

"It's early yet. People are still negotiating. See that couple?" He directed her with his gaze.

A man somewhere in his forties, attractive in an

executive kind of way, paired off with a woman in her late twenties, wearing a crocheted halter top, cut-off shorts, black nylons with holes in them, and ankle boots. Their two chairs pulled close, he leaned forward, spoke, gestured. She nodded, shook her head, bit her lip. Her makeup was dark, her black hair chopped short on one side, long on the other. She was oddly beautiful with the strangely blunt cut.

"He's showing her different rope knots he'd like to try on her."

Monica realized the finger gestures were a demonstration. At the man's feet lay a canvas bag. He occasionally rummaged in it, opening it wider as the woman craned forward to see.

"In half an hour," Mr. Sutton said, "he'll have her tied on a cross, a few intricate knots binding her, and a flogger across her bare ass."

Monica bit her lip and felt something tighten low in her belly.

He pointed to another small group in the opposite corner. Two males, the woman on the floor between them nestled against the legs of the younger man, her arm wrapped around his calf. A collar circled her throat, a leash trailing across his leg and held loosely in his hand.

"He's negotiating the use of his submissive. He might watch or they might discipline her together." Mr. Sutton glanced at her. "Drink your wine, my dear. Keep yourself calm."

She sipped, then asked, "Are you going to negotiate for me?"

He lifted the corner of his mouth in a sinful smile. "I'd rather keep you in suspense wondering about it." He was a sadist. "Let's visit the dungeon."

She thought about the woman with the collar and lead. Monica didn't need the leather lead. She'd already decided that she'd follow him, couldn't help herself.

She wanted to see sex. She wanted to experience it all with him. She just didn't want him to give her to another man. Not before he'd taken her himself. Even after he finally had her, she wasn't sure she could bear another man's touch.

He turned to the right as they exited the bar. The two girls in afterglow were gone, and a man and woman had taken their place, her fingers caressing dark welts mottling his shoulders.

"You did well, baby," she crooned. "Such a good boy for mommy. You deserve a treat after that performance." Then she unzipped his jeans and took him in her mouth, stroking, sucking.

Monica's heart fluttered. The couple might have been alone in the hall for all the attention they paid their audience. Yet there was an element of performance to it. Otherwise, why not wait until later?

Mr. Sutton pulled her under his arm, guiding her. "It's early," he said against her hair. "But things are starting to pick up. So much more is awaiting you inside." He must have felt her anticipation trembling through her body into his.

The hall dead-ended in a T. To the right lay another set of restrooms and a staircase heading down. Mr. Sutton guided her to the left. They entered the dungeon through a wide arch.

She hadn't truly known what to expect, but the place was designed for exhibitionists and voyeurs. The music had a thumping beat, but not so overwhelming that she couldn't hear the murmur of voices from the scenes being played out before her. The center of the room had been raised by two steps, its black floor illuminated from beneath by a grid pattern of colored lights, like something out of a disco club. A metal railing surrounded the main floor, a couple of spectators leaning on it. There was relative darkness except for indirect lighting glowing above the equipment set up throughout the dungeon and recessed lights along the outer walls.

It was enough to see by. Her gaze flitting over the room,

Monica tried to take in everything at once. Spaced out across the raised floor were several crosses, large X's pitched slightly forward, just like the one in Mr. Sutton's special room. Her wrists in restraints at the top edge of a cross, a naked woman moaned as her tormentor whipped a flogger in a figure eight across her buttocks and back. The swish of his hand was almost mesmerizing.

A cross stood against the far wall near the opposite dungeon entrance. Legs encased in storm trooper boots, a dominatrix flogged…well…Monica couldn't tell whether it was a man or a woman, except that the howling hit such a high note that she could only assume the voice was female. Mr. Sutton guided her past a man, wearing only a diaper, locked in a three-by-five cage on the floor, a riding crop stuffed in his mouth.

"Humiliation," he whispered, mindful of the rule about no talking on the dungeon floor.

There were padded tables like something in a doctor's office, spanking benches, wood frames for restraint and suspension, bars that could be raised until a submissive dangled on his or her toes, even a mattress with a stack of fresh sheets beside it. All the stations were equipped with rolling carts containing condom packets, lubricant bottles, alcohol wipes, plus bacterial sprays and paper towels for cleaning.

Three of the crosses were in use. A woman had spread herself over the spanking bench. Monica thought it superior to Mr. Sutton's, almost like a picnic bench with padded seats for her knees and a narrow padded top she braced her chest on. As she pushed her butt high in the air, a man wearing a black mask and black gloves spanked her until she squealed. It could have been the masked man from the bar.

For the most part, except for the guy in the cage, it was men on women. With the spectators ringing each scene, the performers were there to be watched. It was expected, and Monica watched, feeling almost bug-eyed.

The young dom from the bar led his leashed and collared

sub to a sling chair along the back wall. Following them was the man with whom they'd been negotiating. The slings, which were basically full swings that cupped the entire bottom, were three in a row, each separated by a black curtain. Their purpose was obvious, positioned as they were at just the right height for a cock to impale a woman. Or a man, she supposed.

Mr. Sutton pulled her in front of him as he leaned against the wall. His warmth surrounded her, the thud of his heart against her shoulder blade. The beat was faster, matching her own, as if he, too, was affected by the sights, the sounds, the thump of the music, and the scent of sex. As he settled her against him, the ridge of his cock nestled along the base of her spine. There was no doubt as to the dungeon's effect on him.

"Watch," he whispered, his breath sending a wave of heat through her. Anchoring her against him with one arm across the snug corset, his grip forced her breasts high, her nipples almost breaching the upper edge.

Monica watched, her skin hot, her body wet, her senses hyperaware of Mr. Sutton.

The dom forced his submissive to strip down to high heels, garter belt, and stockings. Right in front of the other guy. In front of everyone. Then he hoisted her into the swing and put her feet in the stirrups so that she was spread wide, the shaved flesh between her legs in full view.

Mr. Sutton held Monica tighter. Shifting her hips, she pushed back to caress his full erection with her backside.

Then the dom's voice rang through the room, clear despite the music. "My little whore wants to get fucked." He pointed at the guy they'd met in the bar. "Take her. Make her scream for it." He handed over a condom, then circled to the head of the swing, positioning himself so he could see the other man's cock.

He leaned over his submissive, speaking softly. Letting her head fall back, she smiled, and he kissed her lips upside down. Then he pushed the swing.

His cohort caught the chains, and with one hand, he played between her legs, teasing her clitoris, entering her with his fingers. He was fully engorged, his cock hard and throbbing inside the condom. He used it to stroke her, not diving deep yet, still testing.

"Your nipples are hard." Mr. Sutton's voice was barely more than a breath. With a finger, he traced the line of the corset, dipping to a tight peak. He raised her nipple until the dungeon air caressed the tip. She was exposed, but they were against a wall, far from the center of attention.

Monica loved it, the subtle dirtiness of it, the barely there risk.

"Put your mouth on her," the dom demanded in a sonorous voice. They were gathering a crowd of avid spectators. "Taste that hot little pussy of mine."

His male partner hooked a chair with his foot and dragged it over. Sitting, he plunged his face between her legs, feasting on her, the wet sound of her juices rising to the tall ceilings.

Monica's body clenched. She could almost feel that mouth on her. She'd never thought of herself as a voyeur, but seeing something up close and personal, combined with the hard male body against her, was beyond exciting.

"I can smell your arousal," Mr. Sutton murmured.

His voice vibrated inside her, made the tableau even hotter. She writhed against him, creating the friction she craved.

Suspended, the woman began to moan. Her dom held her head still, whispered to her, pinched her nipples. He pushed the swing gently, enhancing the rhythm of the mouth on her.

Mr. Sutton pinched Monica's nipple, as if playing out the scene on her body. She gasped, the pain exquisite. Her legs shook. She bit her lip. She could touch herself, beg him to touch her, or simply put his hand between her legs. So many things she wanted, needed.

"Fuck her now. Make her scream," the dom declared

resoundingly.

The man stood at the command, sending the chair rolling until Mr. Sutton stopped it with his foot. From their angle, Monica saw the glisten of feminine come on his lips. Taking his cock in his hand, he grabbed the woman's hips and plunged. At the same moment, her dom shoved the swing forward, and she screamed with the deep penetration. Between the end of one song and the start of another, they hung like that, his pelvis thrust forward, hips fused to her body, her mouth open, head flung back, eyes closed tightly in ecstasy or pain. The collective breath held, watched, drank it all in, then the moment broke as the music blared again. Plunging, thrusting, swinging, the two men worked the woman between them into a frenzy. She wailed, shouted, screamed. The grunts, groans, and slap of flesh on flesh sang out to the rock-and-roll beat.

Mr. Sutton lifted Monica's skirt, sliding his hand up her thigh to the bare flesh at the top of her stocking. He stroked the lacy edge, teased her. She rubbed her butt against his cock. She felt eyes on her. A man. Two men. Watching the twitch of Mr. Sutton's hand beneath the skirt, the swish of her hips along the ridge of his cock, the peak of her nipple above the corset.

She was going to come, and he hadn't even touched her pussy yet. When the woman on the swing began to wail in climax, Monica felt her body tighten, convulse, and spin out of control.

"Sweet little pussy. So hot and wet." His voice in her ear, his hand on her thigh, his breath against her hair. The greedy eyes devouring her.

God, yes. She came without even needing his fingers between her legs.

CHAPTER FIFTEEN

Monica had barely come down from the high, and she was ready for more.

"I see you want to be a dirty bitch tonight," Mr. Sutton murmured, his arm wrapped around her, a hand under her skirt. No, not Mr. Sutton. Rance. She wanted to think of him as Rance. His name, even used only in her mind, gave her a claim on him. It made him hers. Rance was doing these things to her. Rance touched her. Rance made her come.

She tipped her head until her lips were only a whisper from his. "How dirty do you want me to be?"

A low, hungry growl rumbled in his throat. With a quick switch of positions, he imprisoned her wrist and led her back past the caged man wearing a diaper. Rance grabbed two café-style wooden chairs, holding them back to back. Climbing the two short steps to the central raised floor, he set the chairs down one behind the other.

"Sit," he ordered, his voice loud and stern.

They were in play now, no longer spectators, and were allowed to speak. On the dais, she was displayed as if they were on a stage. They could be seen from the spanking benches, the slings, the suspension frame. And by the voyeurs hugging the metal railing around the floor. One of the spectators was the handsome older man of *like mind*, whom Rance had saluted in the bar. She realized now that it had been his gaze devouring her as Rance put his hand under her skirt.

Monica sat, just as she'd been ordered to. Rance fell in behind her, spreading his legs around her. Despite the chair back between them, she felt totally captured. Deliciously his.

His breath wafted across her nape as he leaned close. "This is our scene. Do you need to negotiate what happens?"

He was giving her a choice. But it would be infinitely better if he surprised her. She knew she'd have to perform. He might make her suck his cock. He could lift her skirt and spank her bare ass for the audience. He could tie her to one of the crosses and flog her.

Or he might give her to another man and hold her while she was fucked in the swing.

Her gaze slid to the man from the bar. Had the salute meant something? A suggestion? A promise?

Did she want to open herself up to anything Rance required of her? He was giving her the chance to negotiate. Her heart beat fast and hard in her chest. There were so many possibilities laid out before her. Was there one she wouldn't do for him?

"No negotiation," she whispered. Because she'd do anything. The more she gave him, the more he would need her.

"Then you accept whatever I chose." He flatly stated their agreement.

"Yes, I accept." He would make it good. Everything he'd planned for her so far had been terribly good, totally hot. Even if her nerves rattled.

"I want you to get fucked." The last word carried across the floor.

Monica could feel the men crowd in, salivating. She feared her voice might crack. "Who?"

"Afraid I'll feed you a piece of dog meat?" he said in a

low voice.

"No." Yes. Terrified.

"Liar." He read right through the quaking of her body.

Leaning close, he nipped the sensitive flesh between her shoulder and neck, marking her. "I'm feeling magnanimous. I'll let you choose. Any man you want."

She wanted him. If she did this for him now, perhaps she could demand her reward later. Maybe she could command *him*.

"Do you want someone young?" With a lift of his chin that she felt against her face, he indicated a guy all in black. He was twenty-five at most, muscled like a body builder, his dark hair hanging to his shoulders, s snake tattoo coiled around his arm.

"Not so young," she said. Or so coarse.

He twined his finger in her hair, tugged her head to the left. "A little older." This one had been sitting on the end of the corner group. Slacks and a shirt. He was normal. Like an accountant or a middle manager. He probably had the requisite wife, white picket fence, and two-point-five kids.

"Too ordinary," she said.

"All right. You can have anyone you want." He pointed out beefcakes, tattoos, businessmen, punk rockers, hulks, even the dom and the man who'd fucked his submissive. Until finally he tilted his chin at the older gentleman along the rail.

This was the man Rance wanted her to have. They'd probably prearranged it. His hair was an attractive silver, and, like Rance, he was older, well kept, toned, handsome, virile, and authoritative. Of them all, this man would be the easiest to pretend with. She could close her eyes and tell herself he was Rance. Breathing in the spicy air around them, she would smell Rance.

And Rance could imagine he was the man fucking her.

"Pick one. Fuck him. Do it for me. Because I want it. Because you need it. Because you're compelled to please me." His voice in her ear seduced her. She was wet, her nipples tight beads, her legs weak with need.

He raised his voice only slightly, but the next words seem to ring out for everyone to hear. "Who do you want to fuck, my sweet, beautiful, dirty little slut?"

Him. None of the others. Not even the man he'd obviously selected.

"Anyone I want?"

"Yes. All you have to do is chose." He made no exclusions.

She could have exactly the man she wanted. "I chose you."

He stilled behind her, his breath caressing her nape. Then he whispered, "Done."

⟨≈⟩

"I suppose I should have checked my wording more closely."

Rance steeped himself in the sweet perfume of her skin, wanting her badly. Fucking her, though, would give her the upper hand. If it weren't for the fact that she'd tricked him. Apparently.

That gave her the illusion of power. And it gave him the out he craved.

"Do you want to renegotiate?" her voice was softly tentative.

Like hell. "That would be cheating. I was careless. I pay the price. I don't get to watch." But he would feel her tight body snug around him. He would bury himself so deep inside her that they would feel like one. He could watch another time. "So what's your pleasure?"

She stood, pushed her chair aside, and moved between his legs, putting her hands on his shoulders.

Christ, she was fucking gorgeous. The red satin corset turned her skin a glowing crimson. Her nipples peeking just above the satin were tight and cherry dark. His mouth watered.

"Taste me," she ordered.

His sweet Miss Dawson wanted to take charge. As much as he liked his authority, there was great pleasure in following her instructions. Curling his fingers around her waist, he dragged her close, her succulent nipples beckoning. He took one honeyed peak in his mouth and sucked.

She moaned, and her body quivered in his hands. The sweet scent of her arousal swirled in the air around him. Tantalizing. Mesmerizing. His cock was hard. His balls ached.

He bit her.

She spasmed in his hands, her fingers digging into his shoulders right through the shirt. He lifted his head to look at her. Her bottom lip was plump and red between her teeth. Her nostrils flared slightly like a fine race horse. Her hazel eyes were jungle dark.

"Do it again," she whispered.

He kissed the other nipple. And nipped her harder than before.

Her head fell back. Her legs moved restlessly. A tiny groan vibrated in her throat.

"What do you want now?" He no longer spoke to the crowd, only to her.

She shook her shoulders, came back to herself, parted her luscious lips a long moment, capturing him with her gaze. She quite simply ate him up with her eyes, promised more than he could ever have imagined. Oh fucking hell, yes, letting her take her charge was amazing. Allowing her to choose someone else would have been nowhere near the pleasure. He'd had George in the wings just in case. They were similar in looks, bearing, and age. But this surpassed anything he could have felt watching her depths plumbed by another man.

"I'm going to straddle your lap," she told him and stepped back to let him close his legs.

His hands never fell from her waist. She had him, but he

had her as well.

She came down onto his lap, the skirt flaring around him. Naked beneath the material, she nestled her hot little pussy against him. Her heat was like a brand. Spontaneous combustion. Rance dropped his hands to her ass and rubbed her hard against his length.

"That's very nice," she said in a husky, seductive note he'd never heard from her before.

"Do you like being watched?" He needed to gauge the effect of the scene on her. He wanted the play and their audience to enhance the pleasure, make her burn hotter.

Looping her arms around his neck, she tongued his ear. It was so damn good he actually shivered. Then she blew a warmth breath and said, "It makes me wet to think about them seeing your cock slide inside me. I'm breathless imagining all those men needing to touch themselves because I make them so hot as I fuck you."

He curled his fingers into fists, his entire body coiling, tightening.

"Isn't that what you want?" she asked mildly. "Wetter than I've ever been. Hotter. Needier. Willing to do anything. Loving all those eyes on me. On us."

"Fuck yes."

"Beg me," she demanded.

He never begged. "Is that part of our scene?"

"If it's the only way you'll do it, then yes, it's part of the scene."

He let himself go. "Fuck me, please. Ride me. Make me come deep inside you."

She hissed out a breath. "That was perfect. You deserve a little reward." She gripped his head in her hands and took his mouth.

He'd kissed her before. Hadn't he? Yes, in the car. But that had been fast and hard. This was slow and sweet. Her lips caressed his, her tongue tasting him. His mouth opened almost involuntarily to let her in. Then she simply consumed him. Her body rocked gently, her pussy like a matching kiss along his cock. She went deep, angling, turning, tasting, backing off again until they were just lips on lips. He ached for her possession.

He'd never loved kissing. It was a reward he sometimes granted or a punishment he delivered. It was a thing he denied or a tool with which to control.

She made it a seductive act in and of itself, taking him again, sweeping her tongue into his mouth. She stole his breath. He groaned. She was that fucking luscious. His arms enfolded her, trapped her against him, but she was still the one who owned him now.

He could have kissed her all night long. He needed nothing more, the moment so intimate they could have been alone in a vast empty warehouse.

Until she ended the kiss and leaned back, bracing her hands on his shoulders. Her nipples were tempting morsels begging for his mouth, but he'd turned the show over and all the moves now belonged to her.

"You're dying to be inside me," she murmured.

"Fuck yes." Nothing else existed but the need to fill her.

She reached between them, palmed his cock, rubbed him. "You told me to choose anyone I wanted because you were dying for me to choose you."

"Yes." Of course. He didn't make mistakes. He didn't do anything without intention. But he could always take that *yes* back later. If he wanted.

She held his pants taut and slid down his zipper. "You're dying for me to touch you."

"Christ. Yes. And you know it." He'd been dying for her from the moment she'd walked into his office five years ago. He simply hadn't known it until she'd opened his eyes with her sexy resume.

"Of course I know." She slipped her hand into his slacks, wrapped her hot fingers around his shaft, and pulled him out, squeezing him delectably tight.

"You want to put this in me." She stroked him from base to tip, forcing a drop of pre-come to bubble up. "Oh yeah, you want me bad." She slid a finger along the sensitive slit then raised her hand to her lips and licked away his essence.

His cock jumped. "Yes. Please. I want it bad." He wanted to lift her, toss her down, fall on her, bury himself in her.

But more, he wanted her to take him. He wanted her to make it slow, exquisite torture.

Dropping her hand to his cock once more, she drove him mad with her fingers. "You're so hard, Rance. So needy."

He was goddamn crazed. He loved what she was doing to him. He loved the hiss of his name on her lips. And he loved the sight of Monica Dawson reveling in her power.

"Do you need to come, Rance?" She circled him with her fist, gliding up and down his shaft, then reached deep between them to cup his balls with her other hand. The combination damn near made his eyes roll back in his head. He wanted to beg for her mouth on him, her teeth, her tongue. He needed the thing she'd done to him that night in Chicago. He needed her to make him lose his mind.

She leaned close and whispered, "Beg me. Plead with me. Call me Mistress Monica."

The music still thumped, but there wasn't another sound. Not the slap of flesh, not the swat of a hand, not the snap of a flogger. Not even a moan. They were the center of attention. Hungry eyes, hushed breaths. In this place, he had always taken, always been in charge, meting out the punishment. She was the only one he'd ever allowed to turn the tables on him.

The whole fucking house waited breathlessly for his fall.

He gave it them. He gave it to her.

"Please. Fuck me, Mistress Monica. I need it. I want it. I'll die without it. Please."

CHAPTER SIXTEEN

Monica was almost faint with desire. With power.

Mr. Sutton had begged her to fuck him. Rance had called her Mistress in a strangled, raspy groan of need. She was drunk on control. Drunk on the gazes of all those people. Drunk on the adulation.

She needed more.

"Touch me." Her command rang out, strong, demanding. "Make me feel good. Do it now."

Rance leaned his head back, watching her as he gripped both her thighs in his hands and slid under her skirt. The material bunched but didn't shift high enough to expose her. Then his fingers were on her, and she closed her eyes with the sheer pleasure of it. She was creamy for him, ready. Squeezing his cock harder in her fist, she felt him grow, the pulse of his blood fast and hot against her palm.

He glided slowly over her clitoris, circled, then entered her with two fingers. Her high heels braced on the floor, she moved with him, rode his fingers, gasping when his thumb flicked across her clit. He played her, worked her, stroked until her breath puffed, her legs quivered, and heat rushed to her core. She forgot all about controlling his cock with her hand.

I want to come. I need to come. Please let me come. The needy voice cried out in her head, but she wouldn't give in to it. This was her scene, her command.

"Enough." She pushed his hand away.

He watched her with a dark gaze, as if he knew she wasn't really in charge. As if he'd never given anything up to her.

The only way to win was to take the one thing he'd denied her.

Shooting her arm straight out to the side, palm up, she called out, "Condom."

Somebody slapped one down onto her outstretched hand, saying, "Fuck the hell out of the bastard." His gaze hard and greedy, it was the older man, Rance's choice for her.

Her pulse rate soared. Now all he could do was watch. And want.

There was power in denial.

She tore open the packet with her teeth. She didn't consider her inexperience with condoms. She simply held Rance's big, thick, beautiful cock in her hand and rolled the latex down. A flawless performance.

Steadying herself with a hand on his shoulder, she raised her skirt. "Do you want them to see?" she asked softly.

His face was taut, his jaw tight, as if he couldn't take much more before he simply slammed into her. "Let them watch. Let them see how you own me."

A kernel of something sweet and wonderful grew inside her. He said all the right things, gave her exactly what she needed. Played the role to perfection.

"Hold my skirt."

He gathered the fabric as high as the corset would allow and bared her to every last greedy pair of eyes. She'd never thought showing herself off could make her feel this hot, this needy.

Then Monica gave Rance the performance of her life.

Taking his cock in her hand, she guided him to her

entrance. She slid down slowly, relishing the feel of all that hard flesh breaching her. "Oh my God, you're so big." The head was broad, his shaft thick.

"You can take all of me. You're so fucking wet." He didn't push, simply held her, a firm grip on her waist.

She stretched over him. "I want you," she whispered for him alone. She wanted to be in charge, but even more, she needed to tell him. "I want you inside me. I need to know how it feels." She closed her eyes as he slid deeper, her body adjusting to his girth. "Every night, when I touch myself, I think about this." She opened her mouth, gasped, bit her lip as she took more of him. Then she had to see him.

He was watching her, not the glide of his cock inside her, but her face, her mouth, her eyes. Something dark and hot and unreadable simmered in his gaze.

"Tell me," he said.

It was as if everyone faded away. She didn't need the audience. She didn't need the power. She needed only him. "I dream about you filling me to my throat."

He pulled her down, his cock sliding deeper.

"I dream about the pulse of your climax inside me."

He held her tight, fully seated, hot, hard, and throbbing against her inner walls.

"I dream about all the ways you could take me. This way. From above me. Behind me. In the shower. Standing up. In front of a mirror." Oh God. So good. He filled every empty space inside her.

"Fuck me." His voice was low, needy, only for her. "I want it bad. I've jerked off to it. Come to it. Cried out to it. Do it." He held her close, put his lips to hers, kissed her softly, close-mouthed. "Please."

She felt herself come apart for him.

She rose until only his crown remained, then he grabbed her hips and slammed her down. Throwing her head back, eyes briefly closing, she cried out.

Climbing again, slowly, his hard flesh grazing her G-spot, she leaned back slightly to magnify the sensation, the corset divinely snug around her. Her skirt was high, and their audience could see every inch of him between her legs. He dragged her down again, and her body swallowed him. She could almost hear the collective sigh swirling around them. The crosses were empty. They were the only spectacle.

She was slick for him, hot. She clenched her inner muscles with each tantalizingly slow climb and descent. Tensing her legs, she controlled the movements, teasing him while increasing her own pleasure.

"Yes," she whispered. "Like that. Right there." She arched, his cock rubbing the sensitive spot inside. Closing her eyes, she let the darkness behind her lids intensify the sensations.

Understanding the rhythm she needed, Rance held her waist, guided her. She let go of his shoulders and leaned back. Bracing her hands behind her on his thighs, she gave over control of her movements to him. It was like the night in his hotel, when he'd fucked her with the vibrator.

"But so much better," she murmured aloud.

He knew exactly what she meant, their minds attuned. "This is what you wanted that night."

"Yes." It was so much easier to admit everything when her eyes were closed. "I wanted you inside me. So hard. So thick. So big. I always knew you'd feel like this."

His fingers clutched the corset. The bones kept her back straight as they rocked together.

"You fill me up," she whispered.

He put his thumb on her clitoris, and a shiver coursed through her body. She moaned. He pushed her to a faster pace. The chair creaked and groaned beneath them, or maybe that was the crowd gathered around them. She didn't care about them. There was only the feel of him inside her, the tremors in her limbs, the heat building until it was white hot.

Then he demanded, "Come for me."

Everything exploded, her body clamping down on him,

her limbs shaking. She rocked forward, threw her arms around his neck, bouncing fiercely, riding the waves of pleasure, one after another, as endless as the ocean.

He growled, held her so tight she couldn't breathe, and throbbed inside her, his climax pulsing, his breath sweet and hot against her neck.

She couldn't say how long she remained wrapped around him, her legs tight to his hips. The first individual sensation she became aware of was the sweep of his hands over her butt, smoothing her skirt down, covering her again.

Then she heard the whispers.

"Fucking hot."

"Sutton's found his match."

"I want her now."

"Please, Master, give me to him for a night."

"Fuck."

She'd taken him. He'd been hers. But suddenly, in this place, in this moment, she was sharing him with strangers.

"I want to go now," she said against his neck, her face buried from view.

Standing as easily as if she weighed nothing, he clamped his hands on her bottom, holding her tight while she locked her legs at his back. Still semihard, he pulsed lightly inside her. They rocked together as he carried her off. With her eyes closed, she could only guess that he was exiting the dungeon. The voices faded beneath the music. She bobbed on him, sensation shooting through her again. Then he turned, knocked something solid, followed by the creak of the swing doors through which they'd first entered.

He bumped his hip again and growled a command. "Get out."

He set her on the counter. Opening her eyes, she found herself in the empty ladies' room. He'd cleared it with that harsh order.

Putting his hand between her legs, he stroked her clitoris, sending shafts of indescribable pleasure through her all over again. It was almost too much, and she cried out.

"Such a good girl for me tonight.

He eased out of her body, leaving the ache of loss behind.

"Such a sweet, pretty pussy." He swiped a finger over her, then stepped back to remove the condom and trash it.

After zipping up, he turned back to straighten the skirt over her thighs. He smoothed her hair with his fingers, stroked the shell of her ear. And kissed her.

It was slow and sweet, not deep, but it touched her soul.

"So good," he whispered against her mouth. He nuzzled her hair, caressed her bare arms. Then he leaned back to pull up the corset, tucking her nipples inside. "So perfect." He trailed a finger across the swell of her breasts. "Are you ready? Do you need to use the bathroom?"

She nodded, and he helped her down, patting her behind as she went into a stall.

"Leave the door open."

She did. He watched. It was intimate, like couples who had known each other for years. She washed her hands. He dried them for her with paper towels.

It was like the afterglow he'd described. Where the dom petted and pampered his adored submissive. That's what he was doing. Taking care of her. She felt special. Wanted, needed, cared for.

Loved.

⌘

Monica sat in the opposite corner of the car, her legs curled on the seat, her back ramrod straight in the corset, its color blood red in the car's dim interior. From the direction of her gaze, Rance assumed she was watching the activity on the San Francisco streets, still bustling despite the late hour.

He was eminently satisfied with her performance. He'd never experienced the like with any other woman. Least of all, his wives. Monica Dawson was incomparable.

He was almost sad that it would one day have to come to an end. He could already feel that she had a little bit too much control—no, not *control*. Wrong word. Too much impact. That was a better description. She had more impact on his daily life and his thinking than was healthy.

In the past, it hadn't mattered whether or not he fucked a woman. It hadn't been an *issue*. He'd never been consumed by desire. But Monica devoured him. She had him thinking of her in meetings. Inappropriate thoughts would pop into his head during conference calls. At night, he could only sleep after draining himself. Sometimes two or three climaxes were necessary.

Tonight had been exceptional, but it took too much out of him. He'd had no distance, no rational mind. The tight grip of her pussy on his cock. Her scent. Her skin. Her taste. Damn if he hadn't become some sort of fluffy daddy dom, carrying her into the restroom, petting her, soothing her. He hadn't raised a single welt on her creamy flesh to warrant such treatment.

She had truly turned the tables on him. It was time to turn them back.

"You overstepped your bounds in there. That will require further punishment." He wanted his hands on her again already.

She jolted, as if her mind had been miles away. Or back in the dungeon. But she recovered quickly. "What? I did everything you asked."

"I allowed that you could choose any man you wanted. I was not, however, on the menu."

"Then why didn't you say no?"

He snorted. "One does not let the audience think a man's word isn't his bond."

She laughed, then said softly, "You've wanted to fuck me since I signed your contract. I simply gave you the opportunity."

He remained calm, rational. "I say when and where, not you."

"If you didn't want it, you should have phrased your command differently."

Yes, of course he should have. If he hadn't wanted her to choose him, he would have done exactly that. But he'd wanted the episode just the way it had gone down. He'd wanted *her*. Still, it was one thing to allow her the illusion of control for a short period of time and another to let her keep it.

"Don't argue. You will be punished in a method I shall decide when I choose to administer it. Be prepared. Anytime, anywhere. It will be coming, rest assured."

She narrowed her eyes on him. "Whatever."

Christ. Her never-ending feistiness made him want to drag her across his lap right now. He'd pull up her skirt and plant his hand on her pert little tush. He'd spread her legs. Feel her heat. Draw in her arousal. Touch her. Taste her. Fuck her again.

He breathed deeply. "That comment just made it exponentially worse for you." He was already planning. A light flogging. A spanking, his fingers sinking into her heat. Perhaps forcing her to suck him off through the spider gag. Or maybe the cross, having her spread-eagled, driving his cock into her wet, throbbing pussy.

He was definitely losing focus. If he wasn't careful, he'd have to jerk off tonight just to shut down his prurient thoughts.

"You're mine," he stressed, "until the end of our contract. And you will pay for your insolence."

She shrank back into the corner again, her face in shadow. But he could swear she was glaring at him.

Christ. He was so damn hard he could come inside her with one thrust. But ceding control to her twice in the same night was totally out of the question.

Punishment. Delivering it would put him back on an even keel.

CHAPTER SEVENTEEN

With last night's words in the backseat, Mr. Sutton had stripped her of every last ounce of power he'd bestowed in the dungeon. Monica had wanted to weep when she'd climbed from the car. He'd watched from the sidewalk until she entered her building and the lock had clicked behind her. Then he'd rolled away into the night. Leaving her alone.

He wasn't Rance. He'd returned to being Mr. Sutton, her boss and master.

This morning, however, after a Sunday sleep-in, she was seeing things in a different light. For those few minutes last night, they'd been as close as two humans could be. They'd shared something momentous. She just had to figure out how to get more of it. She needed to make him abandon his punishment right in the middle and succumb to his need for her. She'd done it once, she could do it again. He had to remain Rance to her, whether she said his name aloud or not. She wasn't letting him go back to being Mr. Sutton.

Sean entered the kitchen with his hand over his mouth, stifling a yawn. An arrow of red-gold hair shot up from the waistband of his low-slung sweats and spread out across his chest. Her short robe and the fact that she was naked underneath didn't embarrass her in the slightest.

She grabbed another mug from the cupboard and poured coffee for him. "Things must have gone well. I didn't even hear you come home."

Sean collapsed onto one of the chairs at the kitchen table and smiled dreamily. "He's got the sweetest come."

She leaned back against the counter. "So he let you blow him right there?" They might have had private box seating, but it was still bold.

"*Let* me?" Sean fluttered his eyelashes. "The guy damn near begged."

"Right." She shot him a squinty look. "What did you do to make him beg?"

He blew on his fingernails and pretended to buff them on his bare chest. "All I did was touch him. And he totally broke down."

She laughed. "You probably had his zipper down and your hand in his pants."

His eyes sparkled. "He could have stopped me." He drew in a deep breath and closed his eyes, turning all dreamy again. "He climaxed right at the crescendo. Just went on and on." He snapped his lids open. "One of these days I'm going to shock the hell out of him and kiss him with his come in my mouth."

"You haven't done that yet?" Monica put her hand to her chest. "I'm shocked."

"We're not to the kissing stage yet. At this point, I might actually have to fuck him before I get to kiss him."

Sean's dance with Jim was a bit like hers with Rance, one step in the direction she wanted to go and two back, one to the contract, one to punishment. As for Jim, she wondered if he'd ever admit to having feelings for Sean. If he denied what he felt, he could deny being gay. He could consider himself bisexual. Or he could simply call it *opportunity sex*. It was there, he was horny, he took what he could get. She wondered what was going on in the rest of his life that he couldn't allow himself to be who he really was.

She also wondered how much of Sean's emotions were

tied up in wanting the unattainable. If Jim stopped playing hard to get, Sean's interest might very well wane. She knew better than to actually say that.

"I'm dying for pancakes," she said. "They taste so much better when you make them."

"Bitch." He punctuated with a laugh. "You just want me to do the cooking. Fine, you have to wash the dishes."

"Deal."

She pulled an apron from the bottom drawer and tossed it to him. He tied it across his chest and was stooping for the frying pan when a knock on their front door startled her.

"Who the hell?" Sean's wide eyes mirrored her wariness.

The downstairs bell hadn't rung so it was someone from inside the building. Hadn't the landlord gotten their rent check? Or maybe the super let in cops bearing bad news? Worse, it could be Mrs. Brannigan asking for a cup of sugar, in which case she'd invite herself in for breakfast and wouldn't leave until after lunch.

"You get it," Sean stage-whispered. "Tell her I have"— he flapped a hand—"something contagious. Like herpes."

"You answer it," she shot back. It could take just as long to get rid of her as it did if they let her in. "Tell her I have shingles." Mrs. Brannigan was deathly afraid of shingles.

"You're too young to have shingles," he hissed back.

The knock came again, louder this time. She pointed. "Go."

Neither of them considered not answering because Mrs. Brannigan had been known to call the super, terrified that one of them had died inside.

Sean gave in with a great huff and stomped to the door.

"Take off the apron," she called softly, but it was too late.

Sean stood a long moment without a single word passing his lips. Then he looked at her. "I think this one's for you, sweetie."

For her? If it wasn't Mrs. Brannigan or the super, who on earth?

She'd taken two steps when Sean backed up and the door slammed against the rubber stop.

Rance. Oh God, *Mr. Sutton*, his fist out, as if he'd punched Sean's face instead of the wood.

❦

"What the fuck?" They were the only words Rance was capable of.

The guy was all-American handsome, with thick red hair and a body that looked like he didn't have to work at staying in shape. Not even the ridiculous apron tied over his naked chest managed to diminish his male appeal. He was also Monica's age.

Then Rance saw her. The short robe barely covered her assets, and the neck dipped low enough to reveal the curve of her breast.

He should have landed his fist in the guy's face. Waiting outside her building until a young couple had bounded out, he'd grabbed the door before it closed. He'd wanted to surprise Monica. But he was the one caught off guard by a man in her apartment.

"Cover yourself," he barked before he thought. Close to imploding, he retained only a facsimile of control. "What's going on here?" His teeth ground so hard he was sure he heard enamel chipping.

"We're just about to have breakfast," the man said with surprising equanimity under the circumstances. "Pancakes. Monica's favorite. She says I make the best."

He could only glare at her. "Who the fuck is he?"

"My roommate." Her eyes wide, she clutched the lapels of her robe together.

"And you must be the asshole boss," the whippersnapper said.

She gave a low, terrified gasp. "Sean."

She *should* be terrified. Rance was on his last micron of restraint. "Roommate?"

She swallowed.

"Yeah. Her roommate." The guy curled his lip with revulsion. "Just because you're some rich hotshot asshole dom doesn't mean you can barge in and disrespect her."

Monica's hand shot out. "Sean. Please."

"I'm not disrespecting her," Rance said with amazing calm. "I'm simply asking her for an explanation about"—his voice rose a notch—"who"—another decibel—"the fuck you are." He breathed in with a tremble, his nostrils flaring. "*Roommate* doesn't suffice."

She'd told this man things. That Rance was a dom. If she'd revealed that, she'd probably told the dickhead they had a contract. She'd exposed their relationship. Violated his trust. Talked about the spankings. The flogging. About last night. The way she'd touched him, kissed him. Probably all while she was *fucking this man*.

He imploded then, his gaze turning red, his fist coming up as if it weren't part of his body, ready to turn the guy's pretty face to pulp. He would have if she hadn't plastered herself to his chest, wrapped her arms around his neck, and whispered. "I don't sleep with him. He's just my roommate. And he's gay, for God's sake."

He realized two things. First, he'd said that last part aloud. Second, Monica had kept a fundamental secret from him. She lived with a man. So what if he was gay? She had a whole separate life Rance knew nothing about.

"What else don't I know about you?" He amazed himself with the note of wonder in his voice.

The fundamental bond between a dom and his sub was trust. No secrets. Everything was open.

He peeled her arms from around his neck and stepped back. She still held her hands out. And the man called Sean still wore the ridiculous apron along with a sneer on his nauseatingly handsome face.

Rance recognized what Monica couldn't see. Sean was jealous. Rance was equally jealous. They were like two dogs fighting over the same juicy piece of steak, not caring if they tore the meat to shreds in the process. It wasn't about sex. It was about ownership. And who was stronger. It was about which one Monica would choose if put to the test.

Rance knew nothing about this man. He knew nothing about their relationship or how long they'd lived together and known each other. He simply felt the threat, and he was old enough to know you always assessed the threat before you went into battle.

He lasered her with a glare. "Tomorrow. Work. Don't be late." Then he left.

It wasn't retreat. It was strategy.

Monica hadn't slept. She hadn't listened to Sean rail about what Rance's Neanderthal tactics. She'd simply closed the door in his face. Sean had never liked Rance. And she was pissed as hell that Sean had egged him on, called him names, challenged him.

A simple explanation would have ended the argument. *This is my roommate. He's gay. We don't sleep together. We're just best friends.*

But why had she never mentioned Sean to Rance? Not even once?

She didn't have a good explanation, nor had she come up with one by the time she'd taken the short BART hop to work on Monday morning. She was jostled from the left and the right, one way, then the other, almost as if she were stuck between her roommate and her boss. She had to admit she was shaking in her high heels as she climbed the stairs out of the station. A foggy summer drizzle greeted her at the top. It suited her mood. Maybe she'd brought it with her.

Would Rance fire her?

Or would he punish her?

With punishment, at least there was hope.

She lost herself in the waves of office workers on the

street. She let them carry her through the revolving doors of the building, across the lobby, and into the elevator. Her stomach dropped with the change of each digital floor number flashing on the read-out.

She could take anything as long as Rance didn't fire her. Of course, Sean would say that was totally pathetic.

His office door was open when she pushed through the front entrance. Her heart stuttered. She wouldn't even have fifteen minutes to orient herself.

"Miss Dawson." He didn't have to yell, his voice simply filled the entire suite.

How had he heard the door? The man had radar.

"Yes, Mr. Sutton. Let me just put my purse away first." *Let me just die first.*

His attitude wasn't fair. He had no right to know about her private life. Except that she'd always caught herself before she'd said Sean's name. As if he was a secret she had to keep.

"Do you want coffee?" she called.

"Stop stalling, Miss Dawson."

The underlying meaning was *Come in and take your punishment.*

She filled her lungs with a deep breath and entered his office to find him standing in front of the floor-to-ceiling windows overlooking the financial district. Hands behind his back, he didn't turn from the view. "Bend over my desk."

She planted her palms on the desktop and spread her legs slightly as she leaned forward. She'd worn thigh-highs and foregone panties. Maybe she'd been trying to impress him, to ease the punishment. To please him.

"How long have you been living with him?"

She gazed at his reflection in the glass-covered print behind his desk. He hadn't moved.

"Ten years," she admitted.

Silence. She tipped her head to him, her hair falling over her shoulder. She hadn't worn it in her usual knot. Hoping to entice him? It obviously hadn't worked. His features were immobile, but the line of his jaw was tense.

"Eyes front," he demanded, tension in his voice. "How long have you known him?"

She stared at his reflection in the print's glass. "Since junior high."

"And he's always been gay?"

She thought it the oddest question. "Of course."

"So you've never had sex with him."

"No."

"Do you tell him about your boyfriends?"

How much should she reveal?

"Do not lie to me." His tone was low and deadly, sending a tremor along her spine.

She hated to admit the little tremor was delicious. Her inner thighs were slightly moist. "I tell him about my boyfriends."

"In dirty detail?"

She gulped. "Yes."

"And what does he tell you about his lovers?"

"Um." She shouldn't lie. "All the dirty details."

Silence again. Then, "What have you told him about our relationship?"

"Well." These were dangerous waters, and she was incredibly wet. She thought about Sean's dirty details. Male on male sex. And the night Sean wanted to watch her masturbate because Rance had ordered her to have daily orgasms. "He knows about the spankings. And that you used the vibrator on me. And when I told him that I had to give myself orgasms every night, he asked if he could watch me."

"Did you let him?" He looked positively thunderous, far more frightening in the reflection than in reality.

"Of course not. I—"

"So he knows everything about us." His words snapped across the room. He didn't even allow her to finish.

"Yes," she whispered. She shifted her legs, her need

rising, desire pooling low in her belly. She wasn't sure how he managed to do that to her when he was angry, except that it was all about anticipation. About what he *might* do to her. About his touch. His taste. His mouth on her. Her lips on him. She salivated.

"That's a violation."

She hadn't realized she'd closed her eyes until she felt him behind her. Smelled him. "Secrecy wasn't one of your rules." He had only one rule.

"The rule is that you do everything I say, and I'm telling you not to tell anyone."

She could have said that Sean was her best friend, and sometimes a woman just had to talk. Analyze. Discussion was the way women figured things out. But she was well aware how unwise saying that would be in this moment.

So she gave him what he wanted. "I won't tell him anything else."

The smack on her ass surprised a shout out of her. Then a groan. The pain was pleasure simply because he was touching her.

"You deserve punishment."

Please punish me like you did on Saturday. She wouldn't say it aloud. Begging would never get her what she wanted, so she merely agreed. "I deserve punishment."

"Lift your skirt for me."

She raised it over her hips, then went down on her forearms, pushing her butt in the air.

"You're wet, you dirty little bitch." His tone was almost reverent.

He cupped her butt, spread her cheeks slightly, and slapped her again right on the sensitive tissue between her ass and pussy. Clenching her hands into fists, she let her head drop, her body tensing on the edge of climax.

Then he slid two fingers inside her. "Do you want to come?"

"Yes, Mr. Sutton." Her voice was strangled.

"Do you want to suck my cock?" He worked her with

his fingers.

"Yes, please, Mr. Sutton."

He slid a digit across her clitoris. "Do you want me to fuck you?"

She was close to falling into climax. "Yes, Mr. Sutton. Please, Mr. Sutton."

And his touch vanished.

Monica almost wept.

"I will fuck you after you've been properly punished." His words floated over from the window where he once again stood. Far, far from her.

"Yes, Mr. Sutton." A single tear of desire fell across her cheek.

"And when *he* has been punished, too."

"He?" Her heart contracted, skipped several beats.

"Your roommate. You will bring him to my house tonight. I will punish you together."

"But—" Wisely, she halted her protest.

"That's the only way you will only regain my good graces. My house. Tonight. The two of you. For punishment."

CHAPTER EIGHTEEN

Rance could scent her in his office long after Monica left. It was completely diabolical to send her off to the restroom to finish what he'd started. At least he'd allowed her the relief he hadn't given himself.

Sitting in his desk chair, phone lights blinking and numerous tasks begging for his attention, he tasted her on his fingers. His palm still tingled with the connection he'd made against her ass. His skin hummed with static excitement.

Christ, he loved the ways in which she played his games, making them more exciting than he could ever have imagined. Reality with her was always better than fantasy. To think her roommate had wanted to watch her masturbate. He'd almost lost control when she told him, his cock raging in his pants. But he'd managed to maintain some sense of decorum.

He should have been sated after Saturday night. He'd wanted her, he'd had her. End of story. But Monica was like no other. He'd dreamed of her all weekend, even after he'd discovered her little secret. Her roommate had done nothing to tamp his ardor. In fact, his dreams had become kinkier. Which is when he'd hatched this particular plan. He hadn't allowed himself to come since he'd stormed from her apartment. When he finally executed the scheme, he wanted his balls to be aching for her.

Yet he'd almost succumbed to her only minutes before. He hadn't meant to touch her creamy center, but need had driven him to it. Her tight little ass beckoned him. Her scent clouded his mind. He'd been within inches of lapping at her core. He wanted to be inside his sweet Miss Dawson in the worst way possible.

He might not even make it through tonight's punishment before he fell on her. He'd never *needed* a woman, but the desperation churning in his gut was like an electric charge to every cell in his body. He could crave the sensation. It could become his drug.

He might very well be addicted to her already.

⟨≋⟩

Yes, Mr. Sutton. Please, Mr. Sutton. She'd begged.

And Rance had sent her to the ladies' room to climax. The only thing she could be thankful for was that he hadn't kept her on edge like that all day. But there wouldn't be another orgasm from him unless she gave him Sean.

The problem? There was no way to convince Sean. It wasn't possible. He didn't even like her boss. And he didn't like the things Rance did to her.

But if she failed, she wouldn't dare to show up for work tomorrow.

Her plan of attack began brewing the moment she returned from the restroom. It consumed her afternoon, and she left early. Mr. Sutton hadn't said a thing, as if he'd known she was off to follow his instructions. It was going to take time and careful planning. She stopped at the market on her way home. First in her campaign, dinner to butter up Sean, his favorite penne pasta with Bolognese sauce and sautéed vegetables.

As they ate, she endured Sean's diatribe about Jim

ignoring and avoiding him all day. She offered strategies. She commiserated. She nodded sagely. And let him get everything out.

Then Sean asked, "So how did things go with the asshole today? Did he forgive you? Or did he spank the hell out of you?" A moue of repugnance curled his lips.

It was her opening, the perfect chance, and the words rushed out. "He said the only way I can make it up to him is if I take you to his house tonight so he can punish both of us."

Sean almost spat out his Bolognese. Then he barked a laugh. "You're joking."

"He's upset that I revealed all the things he and I have done. And that I never told him I lived with you."

He pushed his plate away and threw down his napkin. "Like it's any of his business."

"I signed up to be his submissive and that means total disclosure."

"Yeah. So you totally disclosed everything to me."

She puffed her cheeks and glared at him. "You know what I mean. Total disclosure with *him*. And an NDA."

He snorted. "A non-disclosure agreement? You've gotta be kidding."

There was no NDA in the contract she'd signed, but the lie didn't bother her. "Please, Sean. I want this. Help me."

"I'm supposed to let him beat me so that you can keep playing his sick games?"

"He's not going to beat you. The flogging doesn't really hurt." Unless he raised welts, which Rance had never done. "It kind of feels good."

He gave her a look. "He's brainwashed you."

She should have told Sean about Saturday night when she had the chance. How perfect it had been. How cherished she'd felt. *That's* what she wanted. Now she knew Rance was capable of it. He just liked to get his jollies first by exerting his control, by showing his power. But what they'd done together on Saturday night was their *real* relationship.

"Just show up, Sean. If you don't like it, you can leave." She didn't want to plead. But she would if she had to.

"I might consider it. Only to show you what this guy is made of. Then maybe you'll be smart enough to turn your back on him."

She thought about all the crap Sean took from Jim. On again, off again. Treating Sean like he was a deviant, but using him when no one was looking. How was that any better? Or maybe she was just adding her own judgment on it. Just way Sean was doing with Rance. He didn't understand the nuances. He didn't know how exciting each new episode was. Even today, when she was on pins and needles. It was a game and she couldn't stop playing.

So she didn't make one single comparison between Rance and Jim. "Go ahead, show me. That's fine." As long as he went with her. "Maybe you really can prove he's bad for me."

"The guy's a total dick."

And Jim wasn't? She and Sean both loved the dance, the chase. It was exhilarating. It made your blood pump faster and your skin ultra-sensitive. It made you feel completely alive. "So you'll come with me?"

Sean cocked his head. "Tonight?"

"Yes."

"I was going to fly by the club and see if Jim's there."

She knew he was just keeping her on tenterhooks. "You can drop by there later."

"Always have an answer, don't you."

She allowed herself a smile. "Yes."

"Fine. Then let's do it." Her heart felt like it might leap out of her chest even as he pointed a finger. "But be warned, I'll do my best to help him let his true asshole self out so you can see he isn't good enough for you."

"Agreed." But she'd already had five years to see Rance's bad side. She knew he could be autocratic, sometimes even uncompromising. He loved his games, of course, but he was also fair, always ethical in his business dealings, and very caring with his family. He could be tender. He made her feel things she'd never felt before. She wouldn't give that up.

Sean wasn't going to change her mind about anything. But she might change his.

⚜

They'd used up an hour over dinner. Then Sean insisted on a shower. She showered, too, put on lotion, redone her hair and makeup. She chose the cream corset with the black lace overlay, the same flirty skirt she'd worn on Saturday, sheer black thigh-highs with a back seam, and the suede heels Rance liked.

Sean gaped at her when she entered the living room but didn't say a word. He'd dressed in casual slacks and a wrinkled blue shirt, as if stating that his attire didn't matter in this case.

It was seven-thirty by the time they made it out of the apartment. In the back of the cab, she texted Rance, telling him they were on their way.

His answer was simple. *Take him to my special room.*

"Whoa," Sean said as they pulled up in front of his building. Ornate lions flanked the porch steps. The marble foyer gleamed and the hardwood stairs were polished to a shine. The vintage elevator didn't creak or rattle as it climbed to Rance's penthouse flat.

"Posh," Sean commented with a hint of awe as they exited onto more glossy hardwood and marble statues in recessed alcoves. And this was just the outer hallway.

"Just wait till you see the view."

Rance's front door was slightly ajar, waiting for them, and Monica led Sean inside, flipping the lock closed behind them. His jaw dropped at the sweeping vista of San Francisco, the bay, the Golden Gate, Alcatraz. "Fuck."

She'd been equally impressed the first time she'd seen it.

"And this is only one of his houses?"

Monica nodded. "Yep." Rance had apartments, condos, and mansions in metropolitan centers around the world.

"Jes-sus." His gaze lighted on object d'arts, hand-carved furniture, carpets from the Orient, crystal chandeliers.

She crooked a finger. "This way."

Sean followed her much the same as she'd followed Rance. The door at the end of the hall stood ajar just as the front door had.

"In here." She let Sean enter first. The door whooshed closed once she was inside.

Rance leaned back against it to survey them. He wore all black, turtleneck and jeans.

"So glad you could come," he drawled.

The lighting was dim, enhanced by spotlights over his various pieces of equipment.

"So." Sean raised his hands. "You think you're going to punish me."

Rance straightened away from the door. "The door's not locked. You can leave anytime." He shrugged. "Most first-timers freak out when it gets right down to it."

Sean crossed his arms. "Who said anything about freaking out? I can take whatever you dish out."

"We'll see." Rance turned to Monica. "Over there." He pointed to the far corner. When she was in place, Rance walked to the opposite wall and pushed a button. A suspension bar rolled down from the ceiling. "Game for this?" He nudged the bar, setting it into a slow swing back and forth toward Sean. Leather restraints swayed on each end.

Sean cocked his head. "So you want to strap me to that thing and what? Raise me up and flog me?"

"Not quite what I have in mind." Rance tapped one of the two strategically hooks bolted into the floor, also equipped with restraints. "Don't forget these."

Sean shook his head, his mouth set in a disgusted line. "So I'm going to be spread-eagled."

Rance smiled with a wicked glint. "Now that's the idea.

And you'll be naked."

"You get off on naked guys?"

"I get off on making people do what I tell them to."

Monica could see the fight rising in Sean's gaze. His shoulders bunched. His hands fisted.

Rance took a step closer. He lowered his voice, and she had to strain to hear. "Did Monica tell you everything?"

"We don't have secrets. We're best friends. She told me how you hit her, took a flogger to her, put a gag in her mouth, and forced her to suck your cock."

Monica shifted so she could see Rance's lips at the same time he spoke. "Did she tell you how hard she came every time I did those things to her? How fucking good it felt to give herself up to me?"

Sean swallowed. A tick started in his jaw. "She's taken in by you. I'm not. Big difference in how we'll react."

"Don't you want to see how hard you'll come? Maybe you'll discover you like it."

Monica's breath hitched as a shaft of jealousy shot through her. She'd never been jealous of Sean. But then she'd never had anyone like Rance. How far would they go?

"Fuck you," Sean hissed. "I'm not a pervert."

"Neither am I. I simply have certain tastes." Rance cracked his neck, one way, then the other. "So are you in?" He speared Sean with a look. "Or are you out? If your nerves get the better of you, I understand."

Sean stared him down. "I'm not nervous. I'm in. Do your worst."

Rance had played him perfectly. He waved two fingers at Monica. "Help your friend strip."

She hadn't really analyzed what coming here tonight would mean. She'd imagined all the punishment taking place with their clothes on. She should have known better, but she still felt a lurch in her belly. Sean. Without clothes. Sex. That's what punishment was all about, sex.

Maybe she was the one who wasn't ready for this.

"I don't need any help." Sean unbuttoned his shirt and

tossed it at her. She had a feeling she'd pay bigtime for this later. He unzipped his slacks while she folded the shirt and laid it on a chair that sat against the wall.

She'd seen Sean naked. He wasn't shy. But when he pushed his pants and briefs down, she was surprised at the size of his erection. She looked at his face. He stared back defiantly as he handed her the bundle of clothing. This time she didn't fold anything, just threw it on the chair.

Rance merely smiled. "Grab the bar."

Sean obeyed. "I've done some kink before. You don't have anything I haven't already had."

"Oh, I have something all right." Buckling one leather restraint around Sean's wrist, Rance jutted his chin at Monica. "Do the other one."

Feeling like the magician's assistant, with a twist, she buckled Sean in.

"And his leg," Rance directed.

When they were done, Rance took Monica's hand and stood back to survey their prisoner. "He's such a pretty boy." Producing a riding crop that she hadn't seen tucked into the back of his jeans, Rance flicked it over Sean's penis. "And so hard." He cocked a smile. "Guess being suspended turns you on a little."

"It's the situation. I'm naked. You're a man. And kinda hot, too. For a guy who's almost old enough to be my father." Of course, he had to add the slam. He wouldn't be Sean if he didn't.

Rance laughed. "Power does that, turns on everything around you. Like electricity." He leaned down to Monica, surprised her with hard kiss on her mouth. Her lips opened, and he dove in. She fell against him, sucked his tongue, sighed, moaned. And he broke the kiss.

"Does it turn you, too, my sweet?"

"Yes." It wasn't Sean's nakedness. Or his cock. It was the scent clinging to Rance, musky, sexual, mesmerizing. It was fear and anticipation. It was the burn of desire along her skin. It was Rance's power.

"This is what I propose," he said softly. "I'd like to see you make him come."

Her heart stopped. She was suddenly faint. Surely she couldn't have heard correctly. "You want *me* to make him come?" she repeated idiotically.

"Yes," he said softly. "I want to watch you suck his cock."

He couldn't possibly expect that. Sean was her friend. They talked sex, sure, *intimate* sex. He'd even wanted to watch her masturbate. And she'd imagined watching him do his thing with another man. All of that had turned her on in a kinky sort of way. But this was different. This would change their relationship forever.

"Monica." Rance's voice cut through the jumble of thoughts. "Suck him for me."

Was that an order, part of doing what he told her to do exactly when he told her to do it?

Oh God. She didn't even have a safe word.

CHAPTER NINETEEN

Monica looked just as she had the moment they entered the dungeon on Saturday night, a mixture of fear, dread, and excitement washing over her features. And so gorgeous in the sexy corset that he found it hard to breathe. Her skin was creamy against the black and white lace, her breasts plump, her figure a perfect hourglass. He'd have taken a taste if other things hadn't required his attention first.

He wanted to see her prove to herself how good she was. That she could make a gay man love what she did to him. It would have the added bonus of putting the asswipe in his place.

Rance hadn't, however, expected her to look at him like he'd just asked her to torture a kitten. It was on the tip of his tongue to tell her it wasn't a command. She could say no. He was giving her a choice.

But Sean just couldn't keep his mouth shut. The man had a lot to learn. "Hello, dude, I'm gay," he singsonged. "She's not gonna do a thing for me no matter how good you think she is."

The phrasing irritated him, as if Sean were implying Monica was lacking in something beyond just her gender. Rance knew how good she was. Better than any woman he'd ever had.

So he couldn't resist baiting the little prick. "Close your eyes and pretend it's a man's mouth. In the dark, a mouth's a mouth." He raised a brow. "Monica has one helluva mouth."

Sean looked rather fierce. Which was an amazing feat considering that he was naked, cuffed, and spread-eagled. Rance thought about raising the bar until he was forced to stand on his toes. But Monica was still ringside at their boxing match, and he restrained himself from making mincemeat of the kid.

Sean didn't seem to care that Monica saw and heard everything. "Sorry to dispel any myths, but men make the best cocksuckers. They know exactly what it feels like and how to elicit the maximum pleasure."

Rance twined a lock of Monica's hair around his finger and drew her in. His gaze on her wide eyes, he said, "So you actually think you're better at it than my sweet Monica?" He stroked a finger down her cheek. "With or without the gag," he whispered to her, "you're incomparable."

She tipped her head back, blinked, swallowed, parted her lips. He wanted to sink inside her right now.

"No offense," Sean said. "But I know how fucking good I am. I've had way more experience."

"He has," Monica agreed.

"He tells you about it?" He was suddenly more than curious about their relationship.

"I tell her everything," Sean answered for her. "And she tells me." He snorted. "I don't recall her saying much about you except that you haven't fucked her yet. Need some Viagra, old man?"

So. She hadn't divulged their Saturday night session. His eyes roaming her face, her smooth skin, her expressive gaze, he sensed the importance of that omission. It was too good to share. Telling her prurient roommate would somehow diminish it.

"Do you think I should take a pill, my sweet?" He folded

her hand around his cock. Even through his jeans, she would feel his rock-hard erection.

"No." She squeezed him, then rubbed her hand up and down his length. "You're perfect without the pill."

"Let's put it to the test. Untie me and I'll prove what I'm saying," Sean boasted.

His hand buried in Monica's hair, Rance turned his head to look at Sean. "You mean you want to suck me off?"

"Let's have a contest," the overconfident airhead challenged. "You said a mouth's a mouth. Just close your eyes and see which one of us is better."

Rance stepped fully in front of the suspended man, setting Monica off to his right. Tapping the riding crop on his leg, he surveyed his victim. "That idea certainly seems to have perked you up." He flicked Sean's rigid cock with the crop. Back and forth. It bobbed.

"I told you"—Sean managed to shrug despite the restraints suspending his arms—"you're hot for an old guy."

Rance slapped his balls with the riding crop. Sean sucked in a breath. Rance smiled and said, "I think he likes the whip, Monica. What do you think?"

Her gaze flitted between them, a frown between her brows, and he knew she was torn between her loyalties. He couldn't ease that for her. Sean had challenged him. It wasn't in Rance to walk away from any challenge.

She hedged by asking, "Do you like it, Sean?"

Sean flared his nostrils in answer.

"I think he needs a little more." He flogged him back and forth across the shaft and ended with another two slaps on his testicles.

Sean's pelvis thrust forward. His eyes closed briefly, and his throat worked as if he were trying to staunch any sound. The single pearl of pre-come leaking from his tip said it all.

But the kid didn't give in. "I think you're afraid to let me suck your cock. You're afraid how much you'll like it. You're afraid it'll mean you're gay."

The young man didn't know a thing. In the course of

dominating women, Rance had found a few who wanted their male partners dominated right along with them. He was no stranger to a male mouth on his cock. Which was why he knew that not all men understood the needs of a cock the way Monica knew his. He had no doubt she would win any contest.

He manipulated Sean's cock with a series of swats, not hard, but in combination, they could drive a man mad. "What do you say, my lovely, shall I let him suck me? You can share me with him, your mouth, then his mouth. And the best cocksucker earns my come down the throat."

She clamped her teeth, swallowed. He noted her dilated pupils. Her breath was rapid, and a pulse beat at her throat. Her nipples burgeoned above the line of her corset, tight little pebbles beckoning him.

He hadn't paid proper attention. Because he'd never realized the idea of two men together would excite her. If he'd known, he might have tried something like it at the dungeon. Though what they'd had Saturday night was too special to share with another.

Still executing swats to Sean's cock and balls, watching him writhe in the pleasure he wouldn't admit to, Rance spoke to Monica as if Sean weren't there. "Would you like that? My cock in his mouth. Or he could lick my balls while you suck me." He let his imagination soar. "You can hold me for him, work me in your hand, stroke me while he licks. Oh baby, I'm getting hard thinking about your hands on me while he sucks."

Saturday night had been her initiation into some of his wilder fantasies, the kinky things he wanted to try with her. And this was another level, letting her share him for her pleasure and delight. "Do you want it?" he whispered, seduction oozing from his voice.

Monica didn't need much seducing. "Yes. Please. I want it."

He would give her whatever she wanted. And he would come for her and her alone.

She wanted it so damn badly that her blood rushed through her ears at a fever pitch. Her hands shook, and she laced them behind her back to hide the effect he had on her.

She couldn't suck her best friend's cock. But oh yes, she could suck Rance *with* Sean. She shivered at the images Rance had evoked, holding his cock out for Sean, putting her hand on the back of Sean's head, driving him to take more.

But what if Sean made Rance come before she did? She wouldn't think about that. Not now.

Sean shook in his bonds. The riding crop had done its job, and his cock was rigid with need. He'd liked that little taste of pleasure and pain. And now Monica would give him the feast.

"Shall I undo the cuffs?" she asked, pointing to Sean's restraints.

"I want you to undress me first," Rance ordered. Except that he hadn't actually ordered her. He'd simply told her what he wanted. There was a subtle difference in that. She realized he hadn't ordered her to suck Sean either. He'd said he wanted to watch. But he'd never cited his one and only rule.

She removed the riding crop from his hand and tossed it aside. Tipping her head back to meet his gaze, she slid her fingers under the bottom of his turtleneck, pushing it up slowly. She grazed his nipples, played with them, then finally shoved the material high. He finished the job, tugging it over his head and throwing it.

Going done on one knee, she untied his shoelaces, helped him toe his shoes off, and got rid of his socks. Then she rose again and put her hands on his belt buckle. His gaze mesmerized her. He didn't look at Sean. It was almost as if Sean was merely a tool to enhance their pleasure.

She had a fleeting thought that they were being unfair to

Sean. He was here because she'd begged him. Then she remembered his hard cock as Rance used the crop on him, and she knew he liked it no matter how much crap he dished out.

She tugged on the buckle, popped the button, and unzipped Rance's jeans. Her breath quickened. She turned then, moved to the side so Sean's view was no longer obstructed.

"Do you want to see how big he is, Sean?"

Sean's throat worked, his cock flexed, and his chest heaved. But all he gave her was an offhand comment. "Whatever."

Stepping behind Rance, she hooked her thumbs in his waistband, catching the elastic of his briefs, too. Then she slowly shoved down his clothing.

Sean's eyes bugged when Rance's cock popped free. He was gloriously hard. No matter his age, he was impressive.

"Do you want to taste this, Sean?" She reached around to stroke Rance, squeezing him in her fist as she pumped up and down. His blood throbbed against her palm. Against her breasts, even through the corset, she felt his heart beat fast and strong.

Sean didn't speak. Maybe he was beyond words.

In a swift move, she pulled Rance's jeans to his feet. He stepped out of them and stole her breath just as he had the night he made her dry him off after his shower.

"You're gorgeous," she whispered. So beautiful. She trailed a hand over his chest, the light mat of hair silky beneath her fingertips. His abdomen was taut, his butt muscles, his thighs and legs toned and hard to the touch. She wanted her hands all over him. She didn't want to share anymore. She simply wanted to drown her senses in him.

"Not bad for an old guy," she said, almost snidely, her gaze on Sean.

"I never said he wasn't hot. For an old guy."

He was a perfect male specimen.

Finally, Rance spoke. "You have too many clothes on,

Monica."

She looked down at herself, the fitted corset, her plump breasts and tiny waist. Tugging on the bottom, her nipples popped free completely, hard and sensitive. "Don't you like the corset?"

"I love it," he purred. "But still too many clothes."

She looked at him coyly. "What do you want me to take off?"

His eyes were dark pools. "The skirt. *Only* the skirt."

Just as she had seen Sean naked, he had seen her on occasion. Was this any different? A little more extreme perhaps, but sex had never been a taboo subject between them. They'd talked about *everything*. This was just one step further.

She turned her back on Sean and unzipped the skirt. It fell in a puddle at her feet.

"Pretty," Rance murmured. "Sweet and hot." He reached down, slid a finger through her folds. "And wet."

She shuddered. Being watched made her hotter, wetter. Needy. Taking Rance on Saturday night had been sexy and perfect, but all those people made it out of this world.

Slowly Rance turned her. Sean's mouth hung slightly open.

"She told me you wanted to watch her masturbate." Rance slid his hand over her mound. "Watching me touch her is even better." He glided across her clitoris, and she arched into his fingers, her head pressed back against his shoulder.

"Why would a gay man want to watch a woman?" Rance queried, his tone light, as if he didn't really care about the answer.

"Sex is sex," Sean supplied, just the slightest quake in his voice. "I like to watch. It doesn't matter who. And I was horny that night."

"You must be horny now," Rance noted, obviously referring to Sean's hard cock.

"I'm always horny."

Rance rubbed himself between her butt cheeks. She had never considered that sex could be so powerful, that fantasies could consume her to the point of filling all her waking moments. With other men, sex had been good, but it was *just* sex. Rance had opened her eyes. He'd intrigued her with every mission to the store for a new toy. He'd made her dream. She could fuck him now, in front of Sean. And it would be hotter than anything she'd ever known.

But seeing Rance's cock in Sean's mouth would be explosive. "Let's take him down now. I want to help him suck you."

Rance chuckled. "She's become quite the sex kitten."

"Since you debauched her." Sean's voice was dry, but his cock was pulsing with his true thoughts.

This time, Rance laughed out loud. "If you'd been there Saturday, you'd have been rethinking who debauched who."

Sean shot her a look, and she felt a pang that she hadn't told him. She'd always told him everything. Until now.

Rance didn't seem aware of the nonverbal exchange as he unfastened the leather cuffs around Sean's ankles. Monica had the suspicion he was teasing Sean, his mouth close enough to engulf the hard cock. Yet he didn't.

When all his restraints were off, Sean rubbed his wrists. "You want this?" He reached down to fist his cock. "You were certainly within reach down there. I believe I saw you salivating."

Rance merely smiled. "I was definitely salivating." He put his fingers in his mouth and licked them clean. "And she tastes so fucking good."

He was standing up for her. Every time Sean tried to beat down her womanhood, Rance built her up. Not that Sean meant anything by it. He was simply trying to one-up Rance and using her to do it.

Sean didn't seem to have an answer for Rance's last salvo. His gaze was focused like a laser beam on Rance's beautifully hard cock. She might have been jealous except that the only goal seemed to be baiting Sean.

Rance took her hand, pulling her across the room to the cross. It had a slight tilt backward, like the crosses in the BDSM club, and cuffs dangled from all four corners. Rance turned, stepped onto the footpads, and leaned against the wood.

Her pulse raced. Corded muscles, light body hair, and that thick cock jutting up. He should have been painted by a master.

"Who's going to start?" he asked, completely in control. He didn't even use the cuffs to restrain him.

Her mouth watered. But she needed her fantasy. She'd gotten wet dreaming of two men. She wanted to see, wanted to feel, wanted to know if she'd actually enjoy watching it.

"Sean first," she demanded.

Rance smiled. It was the closest thing to a shit-eating grin she'd ever seen grace his gorgeous mouth. "Dirty little bitch." He pointed at Sean. "Show me what you've got." He settled into his stance on the cross. And Sean stepped between his legs.

Not wanting to miss a thing, Monica shifted to the side. Sean went to his knees between Rance's spread legs. A strategically placed mat lay on the floor. Rance hadn't used it with her. He'd gone to his knees only once, in the downstairs hallway of the toy shop.

Sean wrapped his hand around Rance's shaft and stroked. He held the tip close to his mouth, but didn't yet put that gorgeous cock between his lips. "Hmm," he mused. "Do you like it hard and fast? Or do you like to work up to things with a slow pump?"

Rance pierced her with a hot look. "What do I like, my sweet?"

She didn't know. He did everything to her. She'd done so little to him. She didn't even know how he liked his cock sucked because she'd only done it through the O-ring gag. She suddenly had a terrible feeling in the pit of her stomach.

In the contest of who would make Rance come, what if Sean won?

CHAPTER TWENTY

Indecision furrowed Monica's brow. He hadn't prepared her well enough for the battle. Rance had denied her so many pleasures in his quest for dominance. He hadn't licked her to climax. She hadn't stroked him to orgasm. They didn't know all the right pleasure points, the intimacies that couples learned about each other over the long haul. If he didn't help her, she'd pay the price.

"Monica," he said softly.

Her name seemed to break the spell. She met his gaze and straightened. "He likes it hard and tight. Squeeze him. But stroke him slow."

He'd never shown her. She was only guessing. But somehow she knew. It was the way she'd fucked him in the dungeon, squeezing him tight inside her body and riding him slow at first. He should have known she'd be attuned to everything that occurred between them. Even if it was subconscious.

Sean pumped his cock slowly, his grip tight. Just the way Monica told him to. It was pleasant. Any touch on his cock was pleasant, including his own. But he should have had Monica do this long ago. Five years ago. God, what they could have had between them now.

Gazing at him, she was so damn beautiful that his heart flipped in his chest. Why hadn't he seen it before? More aptly, why had he denied it for so long? The reasons seemed pointless.

"Come here." He held out his hand. She stood at the edge of the cross's platform, but he wanted her closer.

As she snuggled up beside him, he wrapped his hand around her hourglass waist in the corset. Between his legs, Sean sucked the crown of his cock. Also pleasant. But Monica offered more. Rance twisted slightly on the cross, leaning down to take a succulent nipple into his mouth. God, yes, now *that* was more than pleasant. He felt the first real stirring in his cock, that jolt of electricity that only she could produce in him.

Sean backed off long enough to crow. "Oh yeah. He likes that."

Rance could have told him it was Monica's scent, Monica's taste, but he didn't want to give up her nipple. He flicked it with his tongue, laved, then bit down until she moaned.

Sean drew his cock all the way in. Or at least as far as he could. Nice. So was the long, hard suck back up his length. A mouth was a mouth. Sean's was adequate. He held Rance's cock properly, pumped it as he sucked. All very adequately.

"Kiss me," he whispered to Monica before cupping the back of her head and pulling her to him.

He licked the seam of her lips until she opened. He stroked her tongue with his in rhythm to Sean's suction on his cock. She ignited a burn in his belly. He groaned into her mouth.

Sean grunted his pleasure as if he thought his handiwork had elicited the sound.

"Christ, I want your mouth on me," he murmured against Monica's lips. "Suck me. Please."

He could feel her smile of triumph. As she backed away slightly, she fisted her fingers in Sean's hair and pulled him off.

"My turn," she said. "He wants me now."

"Fair's fair, sweetie," Sean answered without rancor.

He stayed on his knees as Monica went down beside him. "I got him so fucking hard for you."

"Her kiss got me hard," Rance said lazily.

Sean held Rance tight in his fist, and Monica took him with her mouth.

"Fuck," he muttered, his head falling back.

She was so damn sweet. The heat of her mouth engulfed his crown. She sucked along the slit, then lifted her head. "Yum. I can taste you."

He'd oozed pre-come for her. His sweet Monica had simply lapped it up. Now she suckled the tip, swirling her tongue around the ridge. He shuddered, closed his eyes, hissed in a breath.

Compelled to see her on her knees for him, he looked down once more. Her red lips glistened as she slid down on him. Sean squeezed him hard, and Rance had to admit it was a sweet combination. Her head bobbed, she sucked hard. Then Sean released his cock, put his hand to the back of Monica's head, and pushed her down. Rance felt her spasm around him. Holy hell, it was enough to make him explode. Then she seemed to swallow, adjust, shift. And took him deep down her throat.

"Will you look at that," Sean murmured with a hint of reverence. "She can deep-throat." He glanced at Rance. "How does it feel?"

"Fucking amazing."

"Who'da thought?"

She sucked him long and hard and deep with each down stroke. Sean cupped his balls, squeezing, manipulating.

"Fuck, I'm going to come. Fuck, fuck."

"My turn," Sean said. Fisting his hand in Monica's hair just as she'd done to him, he dragged her off.

Sean thought he'd benefit from all her work. But Rance would be damned if he'd come for the kid. His climax was destined for Monica.

⟨≋⟩

Monica was breathing hard, tears at the corners of her eyes. At first she'd gagged, until somehow she'd found just the right fit. She wanted Rance's come, needed it.

Damn Sean for stealing it all.

And yet, watching him take Rance's cock in his fist, his lips sucking on the head, his mouth sliding down the shaft, she felt a sharp, sweet burst of arousal. Her pussy contracted. Her inner thighs grew moist.

Rance had been touching her, licking her nipple, kissing her. And she'd missed Sean sucking him. The thing she'd longed for.

God, it was beautiful. Rance's cock was hard and thick in Sean's fist. A vein pulsed along its length as Sean's lips slid down the shaft to meet his hand. He worked Rance's balls as he sucked hard all the way back up, his cheeks concave. Down, up. Over and over. The sight of Rance's cock glistening with saliva was so damn hot, she felt dizzy.

She didn't want to take her eyes off the sight, couldn't bear to miss a thing. But God, she needed to see the effect in Rance's expression.

The shock of his blue eyes hit her. His gaze wasn't transfixed by Sean. He watched *her*. "Touch yourself," he mouthed.

She had to obey. Putting her hand between her legs, she stroked herself. She'd never been so wet, her cream coating her fingers. He licked his lips as if he could taste her on them.

She glanced once more to Sean. At just that moment, he removed his hand and plunged all the way down, taking the cock deep. But Rance didn't make a sound. Not the way he did for her. Sean gripped his thighs, pounding down on him. And still Rance was silent.

She had the oddest image of Rance taking Sean from

behind, doggy style. Thrusting deep into Sean's ass, riding him hard, releasing into him. Her body contracted with both desire and fear. She wanted, yet the need terrified her. She couldn't let Sean take Rance from her. Couldn't let him give Rance more pleasure.

"I want you." Rance's voice was clear, unclouded by desire or impending release. "I need your mouth on me."

Sean gave up without further fight, his lips rising slowly one last time. Then he wiped his mouth and held out Rance's cock. "Suck him. If he comes right away, it's my win."

"It'll never be your win," Rance told him. Then he guided Monica's face to his cock. "Suck me, baby."

She bent low, lapped the salty pre-come, circled the crown of his cock, then fell on him. Relaxing her throat like she'd done before, she eased him deep, then deeper still. Until she knew he must be close to losing his mind.

"Fucking hell." His voice was just a breath. His hands fisted in her hair.

She began a rhythm that matched the way he'd fucked her mouth with the O-ring. But this time her lips were involved, lavishing him with sweetness.

"Fuck me, fuck me, fuck me," he chanted.

He throbbed against her tongue. She rose off him slightly to wrap her hand around his base, stroking him as she sucked. Then she squeezed his balls.

He cried out, a long, harsh sound. Hot, salty come filled her mouth. His body jerked and shimmied beneath her, his buttocks tensing. She swallowed, but he kept coming. Until finally his seed dribbled from the corners of her mouth. She had to back off to swallow once more. But he still filled her. So much. So good.

Until Sean's voice penetrated. "Let me taste."

She wasn't sure what he wanted. To suck the last drops from Rance's cock? It was only fair, and she pulled back to let him. But he wrapped his hand around her nape and sipped the come from her mouth. It wasn't a kiss so much as sharing. She didn't taste Sean. She tasted only Rance.

"That was pretty fucking hot," Rance drawled. "A snowball."

She looked up at him. His tone had been languid, but his chest still rose and fell with his rapid breathing, a pulse beat at his throat, and another tremor shimmied through his body.

"A snowball?" she asked.

"Letting him suck my come out of your mouth. Fucking hot." Rance pointed to a corner cabinet and said to Sean, "Get a condom. I need to fuck her. Now."

Sean looked at him with awe, the same look he'd given to Rance's exquisite furnishings. "But—" He didn't finish, glancing at Rance's cock. It was still hard.

"Old guys have stamina. And I didn't let it all go." Rance grinned. "I saved the best for last." His gaze rested on her. "You need to ride me."

Monica felt something burst wide open inside her. He hadn't come for Sean. And even after filling her mouth until she couldn't swallow another drop, he still had more to give her. It was almost too perfect to believe.

⁂

"I want to guide your cock inside her."

Rance decided he could throw the kid that small bone. Sean had lost the wager hands downs, but he'd been a good sport. Being the challenger against Monica, he hadn't stood a chance.

"Are you all right with that?" Rance asked gently. She was still down on her knees between his legs.

"You want to fuck me? Right after you came?" There was too much amazement in her voice, as if she couldn't believe he'd want her after that blow job.

He'd never cared much about his submissives' feelings. They played out their scenes, they enjoyed them, they got off. They hadn't needed anything more from him than he wanted to give. He wasn't that kind of dom, the one who worried excessively about emotions. As long as they appeared to have a good time, as long as he didn't go too far, as long as they found their pleasure, what more was there?

With Monica, there was so much more. He found himself wanting to care for her emotions as much as he cared for her pleasure.

"I don't want to fuck you." He captured her gaze, wouldn't let her go. "I *need* to fuck you." Without even glancing at Sean, he said, "Now go get the condom." The other man ran to do his bidding.

He held out his hand to Monica. "Come here." He used a tone you would employ with a feral cat you wanted eating out of your hand.

She hesitated only a moment, then rose and laid her hand in his.

"You were flawless. You deserve a reward. And I need my reward, too. An orgasm when I'm buried deep inside you."

She let out a breath she must have been holding. "Yes. Please."

Sean returned, the condom packet in his hand. "Can I put it on?" he asked eagerly.

Rance laughed. The kid had changed his tune from stupid to jealous to awed. Maybe it was the fact that Rance had come like a volcano in her mouth—which Sean knew well after that snowball—yet his cock was still hard.

"You may," Rance said like a king to his subject. Then he cupped Monica's cheek. "How shall I take you?"

"How do you want me?" she countered.

Any way he could have her. "On the mattress in the corner." There was a raised futon bed he'd never actually used. He liked to make his submissives suck him off. Or he took them from behind while they were chained to the cross.

But he wanted to see Monica's face. He wanted to watch

his cock filling her. He wanted to tease her nipples between his fingers as she rocked on him.

Stepping down from the cross, he took her hand, leading her to the futon. Sean followed. It was almost ritualistic. Flat on the mattress, he patted his lap for her to climb on top. When she was seated, he pushed her back slightly on his thighs to give Sean room to don the rubber.

"That corset is too fucking sexy. And those thigh-highs. They frame your delectable little pussy." He couldn't remember if he'd told her how gorgeous she looked in the lingerie he'd purchased for her. That was another thing he'd never been prone to, compliments. But she needed them. And she preened for him now.

So many things to give her. Gifts, but more, sweet compliments, hot words, intense passion.

Sean knelt on the floor beside them. Ripping the condom packet, he fisted Rance's cock in his hand, stroking him, though it wasn't necessary. Rance's cock stood as straight as a flag pole.

"Quit playing," he said mildly.

"Sorry, sir," Sean said formally, adopting an appropriately submissive attitude. Then he rolled the rubber down.

Rance held out his palms. "I need to taste your sweet little pussy." Not want, but need. He *needed* her.

She rose over him, planting her knees on either side of his shoulders, and he drew her to him. Christ, she was sweet. Her juices bathed his mouth. She moaned softly as he circled her clit with his tongue.

He felt a hand between his buttocks, Sean making a foray into new territory. Rance could have barked an order, but he didn't want to take his mouth off her. He lapped, and Sean played, hitting the sensitive perineum before attempting penetration. It was pleasant. And what the fuck did Rance care? She tasted too good to get worked up over Sean.

He sucked and licked, filled her with a finger and found

her G-spot. She gasped, moaned, but her explosion took him by surprise. She locked his head between her thighs and filled his mouth with her sweet juice. God, she was good.

Sean was getting carried away, pushing a finger inside. The kid needed to learn his place.

Rance rode out Monica's climax with her then propelled her back down his body, holding her for one moment to look into her eyes. "Sweet," he whispered.

She was still dazed and confused, and so fucking beautiful his heart hurt.

"Sean," he demanded, "Get your finger out of my ass and hold my cock for Monica."

"Yes, sir." Sean bounded off the futon and went down beside them once more, holding Rance's cock aloft between Monica's legs.

The kid was starting to amuse him.

"Take me, baby." He pulled her down. Sean guided him neatly inside.

She let her head fall back, groaning. "Oh God, yes. That is so good."

He couldn't have said it better. He trailed his hands up the bones of the corset and pinched her nipples. It galvanized her into starting her ride.

Her body squeezed him on the way out, sucked him on the way in. Her inner muscles had a life of their own, driving him mad as she rocked and ground against him. She fit him as if she'd been made to take his cock. Putting her hands over his on her breasts, she helped him knead and pinch as she rode him slowly, as she tortured him with pleasure.

He didn't see Sean move until he was standing at the end of the futon, his hand working his cock. "Let me see," he murmured.

Because he was an exhibitionist, because watching and being watched made his blood rush, Rance pulled Monica forward, spreading her cheeks to Sean's view. Holding her, he set the pace, taking her to a faster rhythm when they needed it. Her hair fell around his face, cocooned him with her. Her moans and little sounds made his blood surge. He rocked her until he was fucking her hard, slamming her down on his cock, the slap of their flesh echoing in the room. Her eyes remained squeezed shut, her lips parted, her breath bathing him with sweetness and warmth.

She didn't need his finger on her clit, she came from the inside out, her body gripping him, convulsing on him, and finally dragging him down into sweet oblivion right along with her.

CHAPTER TWENTY-ONE

Rance had called them a cab. He'd kissed her goodbye, touching his lips to her cheek. He hadn't sent Sean home alone. He hadn't asked her to stay with him.

Everything had been so perfect. A little weird, with Sean sucking Rance's cock and taking that snowball kiss. And hadn't Rance said something about Sean's finger in his ass?

She couldn't remember everything, just the heat of it all, the orgasmic cataclysms.

And that goodbye.

It was after midnight when they climbed out of the cab. She hadn't said much on the drive or in the elevator or when she dragged herself down the hall to her bedroom.

All she could think about was Rance's tenderness, the way he'd spoken to her, telling her how beautiful she was. The feel of him inside her. Then that goodbye kiss when she'd been praying he would take her to his bed. Instead he'd sent her away with Sean.

She didn't know how she felt or what any of it meant. She didn't know if she'd be able to get up in the morning and go to work. She didn't know if she could face Rance.

She wasn't even sure she could face Sean.

Her door opened. Feet padded lightly across the carpet.

Then the bed dipped, and Sean crawled across the mattress.

"Now that was hot. Totally." He flopped down by her side.

She had an overpowering urge to stuff her head under the covers and completely ignore him. But she'd begged him to go, and she'd let Rance say all manner of snide things to him. Then she'd stripped him to bare skin and cuffed him to a suspension bar. So she owed him.

"Are we okay after all that?" Her voice came out tremulous. "You're not all weirded out and embarrassed?"

He laughed. "Fuck no. I came so hard I thought I popped a blood vessel."

She was glad it was dark and he couldn't see her face.

"Are you embarrassed?" he asked.

She drew in a deep breath and exhaled before saying, "I'm not sure."

"He's hot. I actually had fun. I didn't think I would."

She smiled despite herself. "You like the fact that he could come twice so close together."

"I was totally impressed. I don't think he's actually bisexual, though."

"Bisexual?" she echoed.

"Yeah. He's just plain sexual." She felt Sean shift onto his back beside her. "He let me suck him because it suited him. If he wanted to, he'd have come in my mouth. But he was more about the game, if you know what I mean."

Yes, Rance was all about the game. He'd played them both tonight. He'd even made her feel special, that she was more to him than all the others. Only to have him send her home with nothing more than a peck on the cheek.

She didn't want to start thinking about it or the question would keep her awake all night. "So wasn't that like cheating on Jim?"

"He has to be my boyfriend before I can cheat on him." Scorn laced his voice. "We're not even dating."

"I'm sorry."

"That's what I like about your Mr. Sutton. He didn't

care. It was just sex. He didn't make a big deal out of it."

Her body cringed involuntarily. *It was just sex.*

"I could play with you two again, if you're game."

Oh God, never again. Not with that ending to the night. "That was probably a one-time thing."

"Bet you could convince him."

"Sean." She stopped. She didn't want to hurt him. "I don't think I want to do it again. I mean, we're friends. And I don't want it to be all weird between us."

He was quiet a moment before saying, "It was just sex. It wasn't a big deal."

She wanted to scream at him, shout how big a deal it was to her, but she bit her lip to keep it all in. She bit down until finally she couldn't keep her mouth shut or her feelings tamped. "I want a big deal, Sean. I want him to be with me. Not for two months. Not as his submissive. Not as just some plaything."

If she'd thought Sean would fold her into his arms, let her cry it out, and tell her everything would be all right, she'd have been disappointed.

Sean, true to form, started in on the same old lines he used before. "I always told you he was an asshole."

She put her finger to the corner of her eye and held in the teardrop. "I know. You never liked the way he treated me. You always thought I was his doormat," she repeated his past words in a dry tone. "Well, you were right."

A car drove by on the street outside. A puppy yipped. A front door slammed. She tried not to sniff and let Sean know she was close to crying.

"No one's ever been good enough for you," he whispered into the night. "I just want you to be happy."

Now she really was going to cry at the tenderness in his voice. "I know you do." She reached for his hand and found it in the darkness.

"Sometimes I'm afraid you'll leave me for a total loser. I couldn't bear that. He's gotta be worthy of you."

She laughed but ended on a snuffle. "I'm never going to

leave you. We're BFFs."

"Not a lot of men will let you be friends with a gay guy. Most of them are too homophobic." Despite his dry tone, she wondered at his sudden seriousness and honesty as he said, "I know I'm kind of hard on you sometimes about the guys you've dated."

"Sometimes?" she couldn't resist adding.

"Okay, a lot." Like *all* the time, she thought but didn't interrupt him. "It's because I care about you," he said. She squeezed his hand and let him go on. "I never thought I'd say this about your boss. I always thought he was a total dickhead. But now I'm not so sure."

"You mean because he played your game and you figured out he wasn't homophobic?"

"No. Because of the way he looked at you."

She fell so still she could hear her heart beat in her ears. In the smallest of voices, she asked, "How did he look at me?"

"The same way you look at him, sweetie. Exactly the same way."

They lay in silence a long moment.

Until she simply couldn't help the denial. "I don't look at him in any special way."

Sean snorted. "You're in love with him. It's written all over you. When you touch him, it's like you're touching a Greek god or something."

She could only hold her breath, waiting. When he didn't say it, she was forced to ask. "And you think that's how he looks at me?"

"Oh sweetie, you're such an idiot. You can't see. You don't even know how to look. But another guy knows. When he was making love to you—"

"He certainly didn't make love to me." It hurt to even consider Sean's sentiments because she wanted it so badly. But after Rance's goodbye kiss, she doubted *making love* was something she'd ever have. "You're just saying all this so you can suck his cock again." She felt the meanness of it, but couldn't take back the words.

Sean didn't seem to notice. "I'm saying it because you'll never recognize it if I don't tell you. You've been half in love with him from the minute you started working for him."

"I was not," she lied.

"I can read you like a book, sweetie pie, and I know. That's why no other guy has measured up over the past five years. Because of him."

"That's not true."

She felt air brush her face as he waved away her denial. "It's true. And you thought the only way you could get him to notice you was to play the submissive for him."

"It *was* the only way." It had worked, but only so far. Only for down and dirty sex, for BDSM clubs and threesomes with her roommate. Not for anything real.

"It worked big time. That guy looked at you like he could never have enough of you." He sighed. "Do you know what I'd give to have someone look at me that way?"

"Sean."

"Don't get all sorry for me and everything. I'm fine. I'll work it out with Jim or whoever. And I really don't want you to leave me. I mean, I could lie and keep you here. I could let you botch this thing up with him. Like if you quit or ran away."

"I'm not going to quit." She didn't know what she was going to do.

"But I can tell you're not going to fight for him either. As much as I love coming home to you every night, as much as I love telling you about Jim or whoever the guy of the moment is, it's not fair if I don't tell you the truth. The *real* truth," he stressed, "isn't all that easy for me. But since I'm being honest, you better stop playing games with him and tell him how you feel."

She didn't know what to say. She wasn't even sure she knew her best friend at this moment. Until suddenly she reversed it all in her mind. "Is that what you want to do with Jim?"

"Fuck Jim," he snapped. Which meant she was close to the truth. "We're talking about you. This is your life. Do you want to spend the rest of it living with a gay man because you were too afraid to tell your boss that you're in love with him?"

He rolled off the bed, stood beside it, a huge shadow towering over her. "Do it," he said in a voice so soft it was barely there. "If he turns you down, then I'll still be here with a shoulder to cry on. In fact, I want him to turn you down so we'll still have each other. But I know what he's going to say."

She wasn't sure at all. She didn't have Sean's confidence. She had a feeling she'd need both shoulders to cry on and a whole box of tissues as well. She'd also need a newspaper so she could go through all the job postings.

꧁꧂

She'd pretended confidence for Sean's sake. In the morning, he was back to his usual acerbic self.

She hadn't made a decision about what she'd do, not even by the end of her short train ride. It didn't help that she was so tired she had trouble keeping her eyes open.

Rance, however, was all bright-eyed and bushy-tailed when he arrived, and so handsome, her chest tightened. He breathed deeply. "My dear Miss Dawson, your coffee is ambrosia."

"I'll bring you a cup," she said automatically.

"Bring one for yourself, too," he said magnanimously.

She brought two coffees and her notepad. Sitting, she balanced the tablet on her knee, pen poised, and started with, "You've got a conference call with—"

He held up a hand. "We can talk about that later. First, we need to discuss our contract."

"Our contract?" She knew exactly which contract he was referring to.

Opening his right-hand desk drawer with the hanging

files in it, he withdrew a folder. After laying it on his desk, he tapped the cover. "*This* contract." Opening the file, he removed the single sheet of paper it contained. "It no longer works, Miss Dawson."

Sean was wrong. Even hot sex wasn't enough for Rance. He was ending it all now.

"But I don't want—"

He held up a hand. "I know this will sound autocratic, but that's the kind of man I am. You're free to disagree after I've had my say."

He was going to fire her. He'd say what a mistake it had been. He'd say—

She stopped herself right there. She was a total pathetic wimp. She hadn't even made a play for this man—whom she'd been lusting after for five years—until *he* decided he wanted a new submissive. He'd dictated the terms of their contract, few as they may have been, and she'd been playing his games ever since. And she just…let him. Like a wimp. Now he was going to fire her without even giving her a say until *after* he'd had his.

Well, no damn way.

"No," she said, quite pleased with the defiance in her tone. "You can't have your say. I'll go first." Suddenly her brain was sucked dry of every thought. "This is what I want." What did she want? "I want."

"Yes, Miss Dawson?" he said with infuriating politeness.

She knew the first thing she didn't want. "I don't want to be Miss Dawson to you anymore."

He raised a brow. He was so cocky she could almost believe he was laughing at her.

"And I don't want a contract." She swallowed. "I don't want to be your submissive." She was breathing too fast. If she wasn't careful, she'd hyperventilate. But Sean was right. It had to be said. Or she'd never know. "I want to be your date." No, that wasn't right. "I want to be your girlfriend."

"Girlfriend?" he repeated. Not with horror. Or even stupefaction. "Is that all you want?"

I want you to love me. She had courage, but not *that* much courage. "I would like a relationship that isn't dom-sub or boss-employee."

"Man and woman? Lovers?" He was no longer cocky. He appeared quite serious.

"Lovers."

"Lovers. To me"—he put his fingers to his chest—"that implies secrecy. An affair. We're already having an affair."

She shook her head slowly. "I don't want an affair. And I don't want secrecy. I want to be someone to you."

"You *are* someone to me," he said with earnestness. "Would you like to know what I want?"

The question was gentle, oddly helpful. As if he was trying to take a burden off her. "Yes." No. What he wanted actually terrified her.

He picked up the contract once more, tore it in half, crumpled each piece, and tossed them. "I don't want a contract." He waited a beat. When she didn't say anything, he went on. "I don't want a time limit. I don't want to tell business people that you're my personal secretary. I don't want to tell people at the club that you're my sub. I don't want to give you, as my submissive, to any other man."

Her heart was beating overtime. "If that's what you *don't* want, then what *do* you want?"

He allowed himself a smile. "I'm getting to that. I want you as my lover. I want to go to bed with you at night and wake up with you in the morning. And I want to fuck you all night long."

The words should have been coarse and all wrong. But somehow he made them all right.

"I want to fuck you in the office. I want to sleep with you in hotel rooms when we travel. One room. No locked doors between us. I want everyone to know you're mine."

She really was going to hyperventilate.

"I want you to be my partner. In everything. I want—"

"I love you." It burst from her before he could even finish. "I've been in love with you for a long time." The truth spilled out. "That's why I couldn't find a submissive for you. I just couldn't stand it. And I thought if I became your submissive, you would finally notice me."

"I always noticed you, my dear Miss Dawson."

"Do you still want me to be Miss Dawson?"

He laughed. "I don't. But I like saying it. Very sexy."

"Do I have to call you Mr. Sutton?"

"In the right circumstances, that can be extremely sexy, too." He backtracked, as if they hadn't had that little aside. "I *noticed* you the moment you walked into my office. I've adored you since you arranged that first trip for me without a hitch. Everything you do is flawless."

It wasn't enough. She needed more.

He gave it to her. "I believe I loved you all along. I didn't know what to call it until you took me in the dungeon. No woman has ever taken me like that. With your whole body and soul."

She felt light and unreal. As if something she'd wanted for so long was more than a dream.

He rolled his chair back from the desk. "Come here." He patted his lap.

Monica dropped her notepad on the floor, tossed her pen on the desk, and almost ran, throwing herself into his arms.

Rance settled her on top of him, her legs straddling his hips. He was already hard. "Sex in the office, Mr. Sutton?" Oh yes, it could be very sexy to call him that.

He put his hands on her hips, rocking her on his erection. "A whole lot of sex in the office. And in the car. At the dungeon. In my bed." He tipped his head. "I might have to buy a plane, too, so I can have my wicked way with you in the air."

Oh God. He was everything she'd ever wanted. Smart. Authoritative. Funny. Dominant. Handsome. And so very sexual.

Monica kissed him. It was slow and sweet and sensual. Her tongue in his mouth, her breath mingling with his, her body moving on him, drawing him close, tantalizing him with little shifts of her hips, her nipples caressing his chest.

"I have to call Sean," she said against his mouth.

"What the hell for?"

She rubbed her nose against his. It was exceptionally sweet and seductive all at the same time. For so many years, sex and his relationship with women had been about power. The lightheartedness of the gesture was new, something he hadn't even known he craved.

"Because," she answered his question without any comprehension of the impact she had on him, "Sean told me to tell you how I felt."

"About what?"

She drew back and widened her eyes at him. "About *you*. He said I couldn't let you fire me before telling you that I love you. That I've always loved you."

"I had no intention of firing you."

"You didn't? Then why didn't you ask me to stay with you last night?"

He lowered his head and looked at her through his lashes a long moment. "I don't think I'll ever truly understand women."

She giggled. He wasn't sure he'd ever heard his Miss Dawson giggle. It was such a sweet, carefree sound, he wanted more of it.

"You can ask Sean," she offered. "He's pretty good at figuring us out."

"Right." Then he explained. "Sean was there. I wanted to share what my feelings with you alone. Not with him eavesdropping on that special moment."

She blinked, as if taking that in, then licked her lips, waiting another beat until finally she asked, "You won't ask me to stop being friends with him?"

"I thought he was your best friend."

"He is. But a lot of men don't understand about that."

He ran his hands up her arms, felt the tension. "I will want to dominate you in our home. I'll enjoy doing all sorts of dirty things to you in my special room. I'm certainly not going to stop punishing you. I'll want to take you to the club and do naughty things there, too, but I'm not sharing you with another man. You're not a loaner, and no one's ever touching you again but me." He gripped her shoulders a moment. "But I'll never tell you who you can be friends with. And Sean will always be welcome in our home."

She threw her arms around him. He felt like a big fluffy daddy dom who'd just given his perfect submissive the thing she wanted most.

"Our home?" she whispered in his ear.

"Didn't I say you're moving in with me?"

"Noo," she said with great exaggeration as she pulled back to shoot him a mock glare.

"All right, I'm telling you. You're moving in with me. I will always *tell* you what I want," he stressed. "I don't believe in asking. But you can always say no."

"So I do have a safe word?" A smile graced her lips.

But he cupped her face in his hands and said with all seriousness, "You'll always be safe with me. I'll never hurt you." He might spank her or flog her, but that would always be pleasure.

She put her hand to his cheek, traced his mouth with her thumb. "And the spider gag." She bit her lip. "You can use it on me if you want."

His heart turned over in his chest at her ultimate show of trust. "No gags. Ever." He wanted her mouth on him, her lips, her tongue, her flesh on his flesh. "I only used the O-ring to distance myself. Your mouth was so good, it made me lose my mind. But I will always want to feel your touch on me, no distance between us."

She sighed, kissed him softly, then pulled back to pout prettily at him. "But you're still going to punish me."

"Hell, yes. Especially when you say no to me."

She gaped. "I thought that was my safe word."

"It depends on the tone in which you say it." God, he loved her playfulness. They would always have games. They both thrived on them.

"No," she said softly, her eyes bright. "No, no, no, no."

"That's five punishments for each no. What do you want first?"

"Before I tell you what I want, can I mention something about your house?"

He detected a mischievous glint in her eye. "What?"

"Well, at the dungeon, they had a very nifty spanking bench."

This was interesting. "I remember it."

"I think you need a spanking bench just like it in your special room." She wrinkled her nose. "So much better than that table. You could make me knee on it and lean over, and, well"—she gave him a sexy to-die-for smile—"that would be a whole lot of fun, don't you agree?"

She was perfect. Everything he could want. Why it had taken him five years to figure that out, he couldn't fathom. He'd been afraid of losing the perfect secretary, but he'd been missing all the other things she excelled in.

"My dear Miss Dawson, you're incorrigible. I'm going to have to add a sixth punishment. So you better tell me what you want first before I add a seventh to that, too."

She put her lips on his and whispered something terribly dirty.

"That does it. You're going over my knee."

And he gave her the dirty, sexy, orgasmic spanking she'd just asked for. He'd always give her exactly what she asked for right when she asked for it.

~ *The End* ~

ABOUT THE AUTHOR

NY Times and USA Today Bestselling author Jasmine Haynes loves giving readers sexy, classy stories about real issues like growing older, facing divorce, starting over. Her books have passion, heart, humor, and happy endings, even if they aren't always traditional. She also writes gritty, paranormal mysteries in the Max Starr series. As Jennifer Skully, she writes laugh-out-loud romantic comedies laced with a heavy dose of mystery. Look for Jennifer's new series written with Bella Andre, starting with *Breathless in Love*, The Maverick Billionaires Book 1. Having penned stories since the moment she learned to write, Jasmine now lives in the Redwoods of Northern California with her husband and their adorable nuisance of a cat who totally runs the household. Join her newsletter for updates on contests, new releases, and freebies by going to jasminehaynes.com.

Connect with Jasmine Haynes & Jennifer Skully

Newsletter signup: http://bit.ly/SkullyNews
Jasmine's Website: www.jasminehaynes.com
Jennifer's Website: www.jenniferskully.com
Blog: www.jasminehaynes.blogspot.com
Facebook: www.facebook.com/jasminehaynesauthor
Twitter: https://twitter.com/jasminehaynes1

Other books by Jennifer and Jasmine

Books by Jennifer Skully

Cottonmouth:
She's Gotta Be Mine   Fool's Gold   Can't Forget You

After Office Hours
Desire Actually   Love Affair To Remember
Pretty in Pink Slip

Stand-alone:
Baby, I'll Find You   Twisted by Love
Be My Other Valentine

Maverick Billionaires Jennifer Skully & Bella Andre
Breathless in Love   Reckless in Love
Fearless in Love   Irresistible in Love

Books by Jasmine Haynes

The Max Starr Series:
Dead to the Max   Evil to the Max
Desperate to the Max
Power to the Max   Vengeance to the Max

Courtesans Tales:
The Girlfriend Experience   Payback   Triple Play
Three's a Crowd   The Stand In   Surrender to Me
No Way Out   The Wrong Kind of Man
No Second Chance

The Jackson Brothers:
Somebody's Lover   Somebody's Ex
Somebody's Wife

Open Invitation:
Invitation to Seduction
Invitation to Pleasure   Invitation to Passion

West Coast Series:
Revenge   Submitting to the Boss   The Boss's Daughter
The Other Man   Pleasing Mr. Sutton

Wives & Neighbors: The Complete Story

Prescott Twins:
Double the Pleasure   Skin Deep

Let's Misbehave:
The Naughty Corner   Teach Me a Lesson

DeKnight Trilogy:
Past Midnight   What Happens After Dark
The Principal's Office

Castle, Inc.:
The Fortune Hunter   Show and Tell   Fair Game

Stand-alone:
Take Your Pleasure   Take Your Pick   More Than a Night
Anthology: Beauty or the Bitch & Free Fall

Made in United States
North Haven, CT
15 January 2023

31105569R00131